Dear Reader,

Is Christmas your favorite time of year? Do you have
warm childhood memories of family gatherings, tinsel
and sleigh bells? Even years later, when we're all grown
up, we think back to Christmas and smile.

But for Dante Russo, Christmas was just another hard
day on the mean streets of Sicily. It still is just another
day, even though Dante's life has changed dramatically.
He's fabulously wealthy. He's incredibly handsome. He
holds a world of power, and he can have any woman
he wants.

That woman is Taylor Sommers.

Dante makes her his mistress. He tells himself he'll keep
her until he tires of her. Tally tells herself that suits her
just fine. Such are the lies we sometimes hide behind to
keep our hearts safe.

Their affair ends, three years go by. Another Christmas
is approaching and Dante suddenly realizes he's furious.
He wants answers. Why did Tally run away from him
three years ago?

What Tally can't tell him is that she has a secret, one
that will change their lives forever.

Come with me on an unforgettable journey as
Dante Russo takes the biggest gamble of his life by
opening his heart to a woman's love…and the joyous
miracle of Christmas.

Happy Holidays!

Love,

Sandra Marton

Sandra Marton

THE SICILIAN'S CHRISTMAS BRIDE

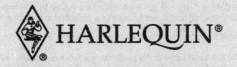

TORONTO • NEW YORK • LONDON
AMSTERDAM • PARIS • SYDNEY • HAMBURG
STOCKHOLM • ATHENS • TOKYO • MILAN • MADRID
PRAGUE • WARSAW • BUDAPEST • AUCKLAND

ISBN-13: 978-0-373-12579-1
ISBN-10:   0-373-12579-8

THE SICILIAN'S CHRISTMAS BRIDE

First North American Publication 2006.

Copyright © 2006 by Sandra Myles.

www.eHarlequin.com

Printed in U.S.A.

All about the author...
Sandra Marton

SANDRA MARTON wrote her first novel while she was still in elementary school. Her doting parents told her she'd be a writer someday and Sandra believed them. In high school and college, she wrote dark poetry nobody but her boyfriend understood, though looking back, she suspects he was just being kind. As a wife and mother, she wrote murky short stories in what little spare time she could manage, but not even her boyfriend-turned-husband could pretend to understand those. Sandra tried her hand at other things, among them teaching and serving on the board of education in her hometown, but the dream of becoming a writer was always in her heart.

At last Sandra realized she wanted to write books about what all women hope to find: love with that one special man; love that's rich with fire and passion; love that lasts forever. She wrote a novel, her very first, and sold it to the Harlequin Presents line. Since then, she's written more than sixty books, all of them featuring sexy, gorgeous, larger-than-life heroes. A four-time RITA® Award finalist, she's also received five *Romantic Times BOOKclub* awards for Best Harlequin Presents of the Year and has been honored with a Career Achievement Award for Series Romance. Sandra lives with her very own sexy, gorgeous, larger-than-life hero in a sun-filled house on a quiet country lane in the northeastern United States.

Sandra loves to hear from her readers.
You can write to her or visit her at
www.sandramarton.com.

CHAPTER ONE

THE HOTEL BALLROOM was a Christmas fairyland.

Evergreen garlands hung with silver and gold ornaments were draped across the ceiling; elegant white faux Christmas trees sparkled with tiny gold lights. Someone said there'd even be a visit from Santa at midnight, tossing expensive baubles to the well-dressed and incredibly moneyed crowd.

Nothing could ever compare with New York's first charity ball of the holiday season.

Dante Russo had seen it all before. The truth was, it bored the hell out of him. The crowds, the noise, the in-your-face signs of power and wealth...

But then, for some reason everything bored him lately.

Even—perhaps especially—the high-octane excitement of his current mistress as she clung to his arm.

"Oh, DanteDarling," she kept saying, "oh, oh, oh, isn't this fabulous?"

That was how she'd taken to addressing him, as if his name and the supposed-endearment were one word instead of two. And *fabulous* seemed to be her favorite adjective tonight. So far, she'd used it to describe the decorations, the band, their table and the guests.

A month ago, he'd found Charlotte's affectations amusing. Now, he found them almost as irritating as her breathless, little-girl voice.

Dante glanced at his watch. Another hour and he'd make his excuses about an early-morning meeting and leave. She'd protest: it would mean missing Santa's visit. But he'd assure her Santa would bring her something special tomorrow.

A little blue box from Tiffany, delivered to her apartment building not by Saint Nick but by FedEx.

He would see to it the box held something fabulous, Dante thought wryly. Something that would serve not only as a gift to make up for ending the night early but as a goodbye present.

His interest in Charlotte was at an end. He'd sensed it for days. Now, he knew it. He only hoped the breakup would be clean. He always made it clear he wasn't interested in forever, but some women refused to get the message, and—

"DanteDarling?"

He blinked. "Yes, Charlotte?"

"You're not listening!"

"I'm sorry. I, ah, I have a meeting in the morning and—"

"Dennis and Eve were telling everyone about their place in Colorado."

"Yes. Of course. Aspen, isn't it?"

"That's right," Eve said, and sighed wearily. "It's still gorgeous—"

"Fabulous," Charlotte said eagerly.

"But it's not what it used to be. So many people have discovered the town…"

Dante did his best to listen but his attention wandered again. What was the matter with him tonight? He didn't feel like himself at all. Bored or not, he knew better than to let his emotions gain control.

Giving free rein to your feelings was a mistake. It revealed too much, and revealing yourself to others was for fools.

That conviction, bred deep in his Sicilian bones by a childhood of poverty and neglect, had served him well. It had lifted him from the gutters of Palermo to the spires of Manhattan.

At thirty-two, Dante ruled an international empire, owned homes on two continents, owned a Mercedes and a private jet, and had his choice of spectacularly beautiful women.

His money had little to do with that.

He was, as more than one woman had whispered, beautiful. He was tall and leanly muscled, with the hard body of an athlete, the face of Michelangelo's David and the reputation of being as exciting in the bedroom as he was formidable in the boardroom.

In other words, Dante had everything a man could possibly want, including the knowledge that his life could very well have turned out differently. Being aware of that was part of who he was. It helped keep him alert.

Focused.

Everyone said that of him. That he was focused. Tightly so, not just on his business affairs or whatever woman held his interest at the moment but on whatever was happening around him.

Not tonight.

Tonight, he couldn't keep his attention on anything.

He'd already lost interest in the conversation of the others at the table. He took his cue from Charlotte, nodded, smiled, even laughed when it seemed appropriate.

It bothered him that he should be so distracted.

Except, that was the wrong word. What he felt was— What? Restless. As if something was about to happen. Something he wasn't prepared for, which was impossible.

He was always prepared.

Always, he thought… Except for that one time. That one time—

"DanteDarling, you aren't paying attention at all!"

Charlotte was leaning toward him, head tilted at just the right angle to make an offering of her décolletage. She was smiling, but the glint in her eye told him she wasn't happy.

"He's always like this," she said gaily, "when he's planning some devastating business coup." She gave a delicate shudder. "Whatever is it, DanteDarling? Something bloody and awful—and oh, so exciting?"

Everyone laughed politely. So did Dante, but he knew, in that instant, his decision to end things with Charlotte was the right one.

These past couple of weeks, while he'd grown bored she'd grown more demanding. Why hadn't he phoned? Where had he been when she called him? She'd begun using that foolish name for him and now she'd taken to dropping little remarks that made it seem as if she and he were intimate in all the ways he had made clear he never would be.

With any woman. Any woman, even—

"…would love to spend Christmas in Aspen, wouldn't we, DanteDarling?"

Dante forced a smile. "Sorry. I didn't get that."

"Dennis and Eve want us to fly to Aspen," Charlotte purred. "And I accepted."

Dante's eyes met hers. "Did you," he said softly.

"Of course! You know we're going to spend Christmas together. Why on earth would we want to be apart on such a special day?"

"Why, indeed," he said, after a long pause. Then he smiled and rose to his feet. "Would you like to dance, Charlotte?"

Something of what he was thinking must have shown in his face.

"Well—well, not just now. I mean, we should stay here and discuss the party. When to fly out, how long we'll stay—"

Dante took her hand, drew her from her chair and led her from the table. The band was playing a waltz as they stepped onto the dance floor.

"You're angry," she said, her voice affecting that little-girl whisper.

"I'm not angry."

"You are. But it's your own fault. Six weeks, Dante. Six weeks! It's time we took the next step."

"Toward what?" he said, his tone expressionless.

"You know what I mean. A woman expects—"

"You knew what *not* to expect, Charlotte." His mouth thinned; his voice turned cold. "And yet, here you are, making plans without consulting me. Talking as if our arrangement is something it is not." He danced her across the floor and into a corner. "You're right about one thing. It's time we, as you put it, took the next step."

"Are you breaking up with me?" When he didn't answer, two bright spots of color rose in her cheeks. "You bastard!"

"An accurate perception, but it changes nothing. You're a beautiful woman. A charming woman. And a bright one. You knew from the beginning how this would end."

His tone had softened. After all, he had only himself to blame. He should have read the signs, should have realized Charlotte had been making assumptions about the future despite his initial care in making sure she understood they had none. Women seemed to make the same mistake all the time.

Most women, he thought, and a muscle jumped in his cheek.

"I've enjoyed the time we've spent together," he said, forcing his attention back where it belonged.

Charlotte jerked free of his hand. "Don't patronize me!"

"No," he replied, his voice cooling, "certainly not. If you prefer to make a scene, rest assured that I can accommodate you."

Her eyes narrowed. He knew she was weighing her options. An embarrassing public display or a polite goodbye that would make it easy for her to concoct a story to soothe her pride.

"Your choice, *bella*," he said, more softly. "Do we part friends or enemies?"

She hesitated. Then a smile curved her lips. "You can't blame me for trying." Still smiling, she smoothed her palms over the lapels of his dinner jacket. It was a proprietorial gesture and he let her do it; he knew it was for those who might be taking in the entire performance. "But you're cruel, DanteDarling. Otherwise, you wouldn't humiliate me in front of my friends."

"Is that what concerns you?" Dante shrugged. "It's not a problem. We'll go back to our table and finish the evening pleasantly. All right?"

"Yes. That's fine. But Dante?" The tip of her tongue flickered across her lips. "Hear me out, would you?"

"What now?" he said, trying to mask his impatience.

"I know you don't believe in love and forever after, darling. Well, neither do I." She paused. "Still, we could have an interesting life together."

He stared at her in surprise. Was she suggesting marriage? He almost laughed. Still, he supposed he understood. He didn't know Charlotte's exact age but she had to be in her late twenties, old enough to want to find a husband who could support her fondness for expensive living.

As for him, men his age had families. Children to carry forward their names. He had to admit he thought about that from time to time, especially since he'd plucked the name "Russo" from a newspaper article.

Having a child to bear the name was surely a way to legitimatize it.

Charlotte could be the perfect wife. She would demand nothing but his superficial attention and tolerate his occasional affair; she would never interfere in his life. Never fill his head to the exclusion of everything else.

And, just that suddenly, Dante knew what was wrong with him tonight.

A woman had once filled his head to the exclusion of everything else. And, damn her, she was still doing it.

The realization shot through him. He felt his muscles tighten, as if all the adrenaline his body could produce was overwhelming his system.

"Oh, for heaven's sake," Charlotte said, "don't look at me that way! I was only joking."

He knew she hadn't been joking but he decided to go along with it because it gave him something to concentrate on as he walked her back to their table.

Eva greeted them with a coy smile. "Well," she said, "what have you decided? Will we see you in Aspen?"

For a second, he didn't know what she was talking about. His thoughts were sucking him into a place of dark, cold shadows and unwanted memories.

Memories of a woman he thought he'd forgotten.

Then he remembered the gist of the conversation and his promise to Charlotte.

"Sorry," he said politely, "but I'm afraid we can't make it."

Charlotte shot him a grateful look as she took her seat. He squeezed her shoulder.

"I'll be back in a few minutes."

"Going for a cigar?" Dennis said. "Russo? Wait. I'll join you."

But Dante was already making his way through the ballroom, deliberately losing himself in the crowd as he headed for one of the doors. He pushed it open, found himself in a narrow service hallway. A surprised waitress bumped into him, murmured an apology and tried to tell him he'd taken a wrong turn.

He almost told her she was right, except he'd taken that wrong turn three years ago.

He went through another door, then down a short corridor and ended up outside on a docking bay. Once he was sure he was alone, Dante threw back his head and dragged the cold night air deep into his lungs.

Dio, he had to be crazy.

All this time, and she was still there. Taylor Sommers, whom he had not seen in three years, was inside him tonight, probably had been for a very long time. How come he hadn't known it?

You didn't want to know it, a sly voice in his head told him.

A muscle knotted in his jaw.

No, he thought coldly, no. What was inside him was rage. It was one thing not to let your emotions rule you and another to suppress them, which was what he had done since she'd left him.

He'd kept his anger inside, as if doing so would rid him of it. Now, without warning, it had surfaced along with all the memories he'd carefully buried.

Not of Taylor. Not of what it had been like to be with her. Her whispers in bed.

Yes. Dante, yes. When you do that, when you do that...

He groaned at the memory. The need to be inside her had been like a drug. It had brought him close to believing in the ancient superstitions of his people that said a man could be possessed.

He was long past that, had been past it by the time she left him.

It was the rest, what had happened at the end, that

was still with him. Knowing that she believed she'd left him, when it wasn't true.

He had left her.

He'd never had the chance to say, "You made the first move, *cara*, but that's all it was. You ran away before I had a chance to end our affair."

She didn't know that and it drove him crazy. Pathetic, maybe, that it should matter…but it did. Obviously it did, or he wouldn't be standing out here in the cold, glaring at a stack of empty produce cartons and finally admitting that he'd been walking around in a state of smoldering fury since a night like this, precisely like this, late November, cold, snow already in the forecast, when Taylor had left a message on his answering machine.

"Dante," she'd said, "I'm afraid I'll have to cancel our date for tonight. I think I'm coming down with the flu. I'm going to take some aspirin and go to bed. Sorry to inconvenience you."

Sorry to inconvenience you.

For some reason, the oh-so-polite phrase had irritated him. Was *inconvenience* a word for a woman to use to her lover? And what was all that about canceling their date? She was his mistress. They didn't have "dates."

Jaw knotted, he'd reached for the phone to call and tell her that.

But he'd controlled his temper. Actually, there was nothing wrong in what she'd said. *Date* implied that they saw each other when it suited them. When it suited him.

So, why had it pissed him off? Her removed tone. Her impersonal words. And then another possibility had elbowed its way into his brain.

Maybe, he'd thought, *maybe I should call and see if she needs something. A doctor. Some cold tablets.*

Or maybe I should see if she just needs me.

The thought had stunned him. Need? It wasn't a word in his vocabulary. Nor in Taylor's. It was one of the things he admired about her.

So he'd put the phone aside and gone to the party. Not just any party. *This* party. The same charity, the same hotel, the same guests. He'd eaten what might have been the same overdone filet, sipped the same warm champagne, talked some business with the men at his table and danced with the women.

The women had all asked the same question.

"Where's Taylor?"

"She's not feeling well," he'd kept saying, even as it struck him that he was spending an inordinate amount of time explaining the absence of a woman who was not in any way a permanent part of his life. They'd only been together a couple of months.

Six months, he'd suddenly realized. Taylor had been his mistress for six months. How had that happened?

While he'd considered that, one of the women had touched his arm.

"Dante?"

"Yes?"

"If Taylor's ill, she needs to drink lots of liquids."

He'd blinked. Why tell him what his mistress needed to do?

"Water's good, but orange juice is better. Or ginger tea."

"That wonderful chicken soup at the Carnegie Deli,"

another woman said. "And does she have an inhalator? There's that all-night drugstore a few block away…"

Amazing, he'd thought. Everyone assumed that he and Taylor were living together.

They weren't.

"I prefer that you keep your apartment," he'd told her bluntly, at the start of their relationship.

"That's good," she'd said with a little smile, "because I intended to."

Had she told people something else? Had she deliberately made the relationship seem more than it was?

He'd thought back a few weeks to his birthday. He had no idea how she'd known it was his birthday; he'd never mentioned it. Why would he? And yet, when he'd arrived at her apartment to take her to dinner, she'd told him she wanted to stay in.

"I'm going to cook tonight," she'd said with a little smile. "For your birthday."

He made a habit of avoiding these things, a homemade dinner, a quiet evening, but he couldn't see a way to turn her down without seeming rude so he'd accepted her invitation.

To his amazement, he'd enjoyed the evening.

"Pasta Carbonara," she'd said, as she served the meal. "I remember you ordering it at Luigi's and saying how much you liked it." Her cheeks had pinkened. "I just hope my version is half as good."

It was better than good; it was perfect. So was everything else.

The candles. The bottle of his favorite Cabernet. The flowers.

And Taylor.

Taylor, watching him across the table, her green eyes soft with pleasure. Taylor, blushing again when he said the food was delicious. Taylor, bringing out a cake complete with candles. And a familiar blue box. He'd given boxes like that to more women than he could count, but being on the receiving end had been a first.

"I hope you like them," she'd said as he opened the box on a pair of gold cuff links, exactly the kind he'd have chosen for himself.

"Very much," he'd replied, and wondered what she'd say if he told her this was the first birthday cake, the first birthday gift anyone had ever given him in all his life.

He'd blown out the candles. Taken a bite of the cake. Put on the cuff links and felt something he couldn't define...

"Dante?" Taylor had said, her smooth brow furrowing, "what's the matter? If you don't like the cuff links—"

He'd silenced her in midsentence by gathering her in his arms, taking her mouth with his, carrying her to her bed and making love to her.

Sex with her was always incredible. That night...that night, it surpassed anything he'd ever known with her, with any woman. She was tender; she was passionate. She was wild and sweet and, as he threw back his head and emptied himself into her, she cried out his name and wept.

When it was over, she lay beneath him, trembling. Then she'd brought his mouth to hers for a long kiss.

"Don't leave me tonight," she'd whispered. "Dante. Please stay."

He'd never spent the entire night with her. With any woman. But he'd been tempted. Tempted to keep his arms around her warm body. To close her eyes with soft kisses. To fall asleep with her head on his shoulder and wake with her curled against him.

He hadn't, of course.

Spending the night in a woman's bed had shades of meaning beyond what he needed or expected from a relationship.

Two weeks after that, he'd attended this charity ball without her, listened to people urge him to feed his mistress chicken soup...

And everything had clicked into place.

The birthday supper. The fantastic night of sex. The plea that he not leave her afterward.

Taylor was playing him the way a fisherman who's hooked a big one plays a fish. His beautiful, clever mistress was doing her best to settle into his life. She knew it, his acquaintances knew it. The only person who'd been blind to the scheme was him.

"Excuse me," he'd suddenly said to everyone at the table, "but it's getting late."

"Don't forget the chicken soup," a woman called after him.

Dante had instructed his driver to take him to Taylor's apartment. It was time to set things straight. To make sure she still understood their agreement, that the rules hadn't changed simply because their affair had gone on so long.

In fact, perhaps it was time to end the relationship. Not tonight. Not abruptly. He'd simply see her less often. In a few weeks, he'd take her to L'Etoile for dinner, give her a bracelet or a pair of earrings to remember him by and tell her their time together had been fun but—

But Taylor didn't answer the door when he rang—which reminded him that she'd never given him a key. He hadn't given her one to his place, either, but that was different. He never gave his mistresses keys, but they were always eager to give theirs to him.

And it occurred to him again, as it often did, that Taylor wasn't really his mistress. She insisted on paying her own rent, even though most women gladly let him do it.

"I'm not most women," she'd said when he'd tried to insist, and he'd told himself that was good, that he admired her independence.

That night, however, he saw it for what it was. Just another way to heighten his interest, he'd thought coldly, as he rang the bell again.

Still no answer.

His thoughts turned even colder. Was she out with another man?

No. She was sick. He believed that; she'd sounded terrible on the phone when she'd called him earlier, her voice hoarse and raw.

Dante's heart had skittered. Was she lying unconscious behind the locked door? He took the stairs to the super's basement apartment at a gallop when the damned elevator refused to come, awakened the man and bought his cooperation with a fistful of bills.

Together, they'd gone up to Taylor's apartment. Unlocked the door…

And found the place empty.

His mistress was gone.

Her things were gone, too. All that remained was a trace of her scent in the air and a note, a *note,* goddamn her, on the coffee table.

"Thank you for everything," she had written, "it's been fun." Only that, as if their affair had been a game.

And Dante had swallowed the insult. What else could he have done? Hired a detective to find her? That would only have made his humiliation worse.

Three years. Three years, and now, without warning, it had all caught up to him. The embarrassment. The anger...

"Dante?"

He turned around. Charlotte had somehow managed to find him. She stood on the loading dock, wrapped in a velvet cloak he'd bought her, her face pink with anger.

"Here you are," she said sharply.

"Charlotte. My apologies. I, ah, I came out for a breath of air—"

"You said you wouldn't embarrass me."

"Yes. I know. And I won't. I told you, I only stepped outside—"

"You've been gone almost an hour! How dare you make me look foolish to my friends?" Her voice rose. "Who do you think you are?"

Dante's eyes narrowed. He moved toward her, and something dangerous must have shown in his face because she took a quick step back.

"I know exactly who I am," he said softly. "I am Dante Russo, and whoever deals with me should never forget it."

"Dante. I only meant—"

He took her arm, quick-marched her down a set of concrete steps and away from the dock. An alley led to the street where he hailed a cab, handed the driver a hundred-dollar bill and told him Charlotte's address.

He'd left his topcoat inside the hotel but he didn't give a damn. Coats were easy to replace. Pride wasn't.

"Dante," she stammered, "really, I'm sorry—"

So was he, but not for what had just happened. He was sorry he had lived a lie for the past three years.

Taylor Sommers had made a fool of him. Nobody, *nobody* got away with that.

He took his cell phone from his pocket and called his driver. When his Mercedes pulled to the curb, Dante got in the back and pressed another number on the phone. It was late, but his personal attorney answered on the first ring.

He didn't waste time on preliminaries. "I need a private investigator," he said. "No, not first thing Monday. Tomorrow. Have him call me at home."

Three years had gone by. So what? Someone had once said that revenge was a dish best served cold.

A tight smile curved Dante's hard mouth.

He couldn't have agreed more.

IT WAS A LONG WEEKEND.

Charlotte left endless messages on his voice mail. They ranged from weepy to demanding, and he erased them all.

Saturday morning, he heard from the detective his attorney had contacted. The man asked for everything Dante knew about Taylor.

"Her name," he said, "is Taylor Sommers. She lived in the Stanhope, on Gramercy Park. She's an interior decorator."

There was a silence.

"And?" the man said.

"And what? Isn't that enough?"

"Well, I could use the names of her parents. Her friends. Date of birth. Where she grew up. What schools she attended."

"I've told you everything I know," Dante said coldly.

He hung up the phone, then walked through his bedroom and onto the wraparound terrace that surrounded his Central Park West penthouse. It was cold; the wind had a way of whipping around the building at this height. And it had snowed overnight, not heavily, just enough to turn the park a pristine white.

Dante frowned.

The detective had seemed surprised he knew so little about Taylor, but why would he have known more? She pleased his eye; she was passionate and intelligent.

What more would a man want from a woman?

There had been moments, though. Like the time he'd brought her here for a late supper. It had snowed that night, too. He'd excused himself, gone to make a brief but necessary phone call. When he came back, he'd found the terrace door open and Taylor standing out here, just as he was now.

She'd been wearing a silk dress, a little slip of a thing. He'd taken off his jacket, stepped outside and put it around her shoulders.

"What are you doing, *cara?* It's much too cold for you out here."

"I know," she'd answered, snuggling into his jacket and into the curve of his arm, "but it's so beautiful, Dante." She'd turned her face up to his and smiled. "I love nights like this, don't you?"

Cold nights reminded him of the frigid winters in

Palermo, the way he'd padded his shoes with newspaper in a useless attempt to keep warm.

For some reason he still couldn't comprehend, he'd almost told her that.

Of course, he had not done anything so foolish. Instead, he'd kissed her.

"If you can get over your penchant for cold and snow," he'd said, with a little smile, "we can fly to the Caribbean some weekend and you can help me house-hunt. I've been thinking about buying a place in the islands."

Her smile had been soft. "I'd like that," she'd said. "I'd like it very, very much."

Instantly, he'd realized what a mistake he'd made. He'd asked her to take a step into his life and he'd never meant to do that.

He'd never mentioned the Caribbean again. Not that it mattered, because two weeks later, she'd walked out on him.

Walked out, he thought now, his jaw tightening. Left him to come up with excuses explaining her absence at all those endless Christmas charitable events he was expected to attend.

But he'd solved that problem simply enough.

He'd found replacements for her. He'd gone through that season with an endless array of beautiful women on his arm.

On his arm, but not in his bed. It had been a long time until he'd had sex after Taylor, and even then, it hadn't been the same.

The truth was, it still wasn't. Something was lacking.

Not for his lovers. He knew damned well how to make a woman cry out with pleasure but he felt—what was the word? Removed. That was it. His body went through all the motions, but when it was over, he felt unsatisfied.

Taylor was to blame for that.

What in hell had possessed him, to let her walk away? To let her think she'd ended their affair when she hadn't? A man's ego could take just so much.

By Monday, his anger was at the boiling point. When the private investigator turned up at his office, he greeted him with barely concealed impatience.

"Well? Surely you've located Ms. Sommers. How difficult can it be to find a woman in this city?"

The man scratched his ear, took a notepad from his pocket and thumbed it open.

"See, that was the problem, Mr. Russo. The lady isn't in this city. She's in…" He frowned. "Shelby, Vermont."

Dante stared at him. "Vermont?"

"Yeah. Little town, maybe fifty miles from Burlington."

Taylor, in a New England village? Dante almost laughed trying to picture his sophisticated former lover in such a setting.

"The lady has an interior decorating business." The P.I. turned the page. "And she's done okay. In fact, she just applied for an expansion loan at—"

The P.I. rattled on but Dante was only half listening. He knew where to find Taylor. Everything else was superfluous.

How surprised she'd be, he thought with grim satisfaction, to see him again. To hear him tell her that she hadn't needed to leave him, that he'd been leaving her—

"…just for the two of them. I have the details, if you—"

Dante's head came up. "Just for the two of what?" he said carefully.

"Of them," the P.I. said, raising an eyebrow. "You know, what I was saying about the house she inherited. A couple of realtors suggested she might want something newer and larger but she said no, she wanted a small house in a quiet setting, just big enough for two. For her and, uh... I got the name right here, if you just give me a—"

"A house for two people?" Dante said, in a tone opponents had learned to fear.

"That's right. Her and—here it is. Sam Gardner."

"Taylor." Dante cleared his throat. "And Sam Gardner. They live together?"

"Well, sure."

"And Gardner was with her when she moved in?"

The P.I. chuckled. "Yessir. I mean—"

"I know exactly what you mean," Dante said without inflection. "Thank you. You've been most helpful."

"Yeah, but, Mr. Russo—"

"Most helpful," Dante repeated.

The detective got the message.

Alone, Dante told himself he'd accomplish nothing unless he stayed calm, but a knot of red-hot rage was already blooming in his gut. Taylor hadn't left him because she'd grown bored. She'd left him for another man. She'd been seeing someone, making love with someone, while she'd been with him.

He went to the window and clasped the edge of the sill, hands tightening on the marble the way they wanted to tighten on her throat. Confronting her wouldn't be enough. Beating the crap out of her lover wouldn't be enough, either, although it would damned well help.

He wanted more. Wanted the kind of revenge that her infidelity merited. How dare she make a fool of him? How dare she?

There had to be a way. A plan.

Suddenly, he recalled the P.I.'s words. *She's done well. In fact, she's just applied for an expansion loan at the local bank.*

Dante smiled. There was. And he could hardly wait to put it into motion.

CHAPTER TWO

TAYLOR SOMMERS POURED a cup of coffee, put it on the sink, opened the refrigerator to get the cream and realized she'd already put it on the table, right alongside the cup she'd already filled with coffee only minutes before.

She took a steadying breath.

"Keep it up," she said, her voice loud in the silence, "and Walter Dennison's going to tell you he was only joking when he said he'd change those loan payments."

Dennison was a nice man; he'd been a friend of her grandmother's. He'd shown compassion and small-town courtesy when Tally fell behind on repaying the home equity loan his bank had granted her.

But he wasn't a fool and only a fool would go on doing that for a woman who behaved as if she were coming apart.

Was that why he wanted to see her today? Had he changed his mind? If he had, if he wanted her to pay the amount the loan called for each month…

Tally closed her eyes.

She'd be finished. The town had already shut down

the interior decorating business she'd been running from home. Without the loan, she'd lose the shop she'd rented on the village green even before it opened because, to put it simply, she was broke.

Flat broke.

Okay, if you wanted absolute accuracy, she had two hundred dollars in her bank account, but it was a drop in the bucket compared to what she needed.

She'd long ago used up her savings. Moving to Vermont, paying for repairs to make livable the old house she'd inherited from her grandmother, just day-to-day expenses for Sam and her had taken a huge chunk of her savings.

Start-up costs for INTERIORS BY TAYLOR had swallowed the rest. Beginning a decorating business, even from home, was expensive. You had to have at least a small showroom—in her case, what had once been an enclosed porch on the back of the house—so that potential clients could get a feel for your work. Paint, fabric, wicker furniture to make the porch inviting had cost a bundle.

Then there were the fabric samples, decorative items like vases and lamps, handmade candles and fireplace accessories... Expensive, all of them. Some catalogs alone could be incredibly pricey. Advertising costs were astronomical but if you didn't reach the right people, all your other efforts were pointless.

Little by little, INTERIORS BY TAYLOR had begun to draw clients from the upscale ski communities within miles of tiny Shelby. Taylor's accounts had still been in the red, but things had definitely been looking up.

And then the town clerk phoned. He was apologetic, but that didn't make his message any less harsh.

INTERIORS BY TAYLOR was operating illegally. The town had an ordinance against home-based businesses.

That Shelby, Vermont, population 8500 on a good day, had ordinances at all had been a surprise. But it did, and this one was inviolate. You couldn't operate a business from your house even if you'd been raised under its roof after your mother took off for parts unknown.

Tally's pleading had gained her a two-month reprieve.

She'd found a soon-to-be-vacant shop on the village green. Each night, long after Sam was asleep, she'd worked and reworked the costs she'd face. The monthly rent. The three-months up-front deposit. The fees for the carpenter, painter and electrician needed to turn the place from the TV-repair shop it had been into an elegant setting for her designs.

And then there were all the things she'd have to buy to create the right atmosphere. Add in the cost of increased advertising and Tally had arrived at a number that was staggering.

She needed $175,000.00.

The next morning, she'd kissed Sam goodbye, put on a white silk blouse and a black suit she hadn't worn since New York. She'd pulled her blond hair into a knot at the base of her neck and gone to see Walter Dennison, who owned Shelby's one and only bank.

Dennison read through the proposal she'd written, looked up and frowned.

"You're asking for a lot of money."

"I know."

"Asking for it in a home equity loan."

"Yes, sir."

"You understand what would happen if you were unable to pay the loan off, Ms. Sommers? That the bank would have the right to foreclose on your house?"

Taylor had nodded. "Yes, sir," she'd said again. "I do."

Dennison had looked at her for a long moment. Then he'd smiled. "You've got your grandmother's gumption, Tally," he'd said, and held out his hand.

The loan was hers.

She'd made the first payment...but not the second. Or the third. The contractors demanded their money according to the schedules she'd agreed to. Things couldn't get worse, she'd thought...

And the furnace in the house went belly-up.

Pride in tatters, Taylor had gone to Dennison again. If he could see his way clear to lower the monthly payments...

He'd sighed and run his fingers through his thinning hair. In the end he'd done it.

Which brought her back to today's phone call. It had come while she and Sam were having breakfast.

"I need to see you, Ms. Sommers," Dennison had said. "Today."

She'd almost stopped breathing. "Is it about my loan?"

There'd been a little pause. Then Dennison had said yes, it was, and she was to come to his office at four.

"Four," he'd repeated, "promptly, please."

The admonition had surprised her. So had the change from Tally to Ms. Sommers. She'd told herself it wasn't a bad sign. A man who wanted to discuss a six-figure loan was entitled to be a little formal, even if he'd known you since you were a baby.

"Of course," she'd said, all cool New York sophistication. Then she'd hung up the phone and tried to smile at Sam, whose eyes were filled with questions.

"Nothing to worry about, babe," Tally had said airily.

Sam had grinned a Sam-grin, at least until she said she might not be home until suppertime.

"You can visit the Millers," she'd said reassuringly. "You know how much you like them."

She'd smoothed things over by promising they'd have the entire weekend together, doing what Sam liked most: snuggling with her on the sofa, watching videos and eating popcorn.

Dante Russo had probably never watched a video or eaten popcorn in his life...

And what was that man doing in her head again?

Who gave a damn what Dante Russo did or didn't do? He was history. Besides, he'd never meant anything more to her than what she'd meant to him. New York was filled with relationships like theirs. Two consenting adults going out together, being seen together...

Having sex together.

Tally's eyes closed. Memories rushed in. Scents. Tastes. Sensations. Dante's hands, deliciously rough on her skin. His mouth, demanding surrender as he kissed her. His face above her, his silver eyes dark as storm clouds, his sensual lips drawn back with passion...

She swung toward the sink, dumped her coffee and rinsed out the cup.

What stupid thoughts to have today of all days, when she had to be at her best. Still, she understood why she would think of Dante.

Her mouth curved in a bitter smile.

This was an anniversary of sorts. She'd left Dante

Russo a few weeks before Christmas, three years ago. All it took was the scent of pine and the sound of carols to bring the memories rushing back.

She wouldn't let that happen. Dante had no place in the new life she'd built for herself. For herself and Sam.

He was nothing to her anymore.

Or to Sam.

Sam didn't know Dante existed. And Dante certainly didn't know about Sam. He never would, either. She would see to that.

Tally knew her former lover well.

Dante hadn't wanted her and surely wouldn't have understood why she wanted Sam… But that didn't mean he'd simply let her have Sam, if he knew.

Her former lover could be charming but underneath he was cold, determined and ruthless. She refused to think about how he might react if he knew everything.

Tally sighed and turned on the kitchen lights. Night had fallen; it came early to these northern latitudes. The coming storm the weatherman had predicted rattled the old windows.

She'd fled New York on a night like this. Cold, dark, with snow in the forecast.

What a wreck she'd been that night! Pretending to be sick, then packing her clothes and scribbling that final note. All she'd been able to think about was getting away before Dante showed up.

She wasn't stupid. She'd known he hadn't wanted her anymore. He'd been removed and distant for a while and sometimes she'd caught him watching her with a look on his face that made her want to weep.

He was bored with her. And getting ready to end

their affair, but she wouldn't let that happen. She'd end it first. It would be quicker, less humiliating...

And safer, because by then she had a secret she'd never have been foolish enough to share with him.

So she'd made plans to leave him. And she'd done it so he wouldn't be able to find her, even if he looked for her. Not that she thought he would. Why would a man go after a woman when she'd saved him the trouble of getting rid of her?

Even if he had, maybe out of all that macho Sicilian arrogance made all the more potent by his power, his wealth, his gorgeous face and body—even if he had, he'd never have found her. He'd never dream she'd flee to a tiny village in New England. He knew nothing about her. In their six months together, he'd never asked her questions about herself.

Not real ones.

Would you prefer Chez Nicole or L'Etoile for dinner? he'd ask. *Shall I get tickets for the ballet or the symphony?*

Things a man would ask any woman. Never anything more important.

Well, yes. He'd asked her other things. Whispered them, in that husky voice that was a turn-on all by itself.

Do you like it when I touch you this way? And if what he was doing seemed too much, if it made her tremble in his arms, he'd kiss her deeply and say, *Don't stop me, bellissima. Let me. Yes. Let me do this. Yes. Like that. Just like that...*

She was trembling even now, just remembering those moments.

"You're a fool," Tally said, her voice sharp in the silence of the kitchen.

Sex with Dante had been incredible, but sex was all
it was, even though lying beneath him, feeling the power
of his penetration, his possession, sometimes made her
want to weep with joy. But it didn't make up for the fact
that he'd never once spent the entire night in her bed or
asked her to come to his.

Stay with me, she'd wanted to say, oh, so many times.
But she hadn't. Only the once, when the words had
slipped out before she could stop them…

Only the once, when she'd forgotten that all her lover
wanted was her body, not her heart.

Tally turned her back to the window.

So what?

Why would she have wanted a man to tie her down,
give her a baby and then turn his ever-wandering eyes
elsewhere as her father had done, as a man like Dante
Russo would surely do?

It was the meeting with Walter Dennison that had her
feeling so strange, that was all. Once she put that behind
her, she'd be fine.

And it was time to get moving. *Be here at four, Ms.
Sommers, and please be prompt.*

She smiled as put on her coat and grabbed her car
keys. All those years in New York had made her forget
how pedantic a true Yankee could be.

As USUAL, the weatherman had it wrong. Snow was
already falling as if someone were shaking a featherbed
over the town.

The snow dusting the woods and fields with a blanket
of white as Tally drove past would have made a beautiful Christmas card. In the real world, it made for a dan-

gerous drive. The narrow road that led into the heart of town already wore a thin coating of black ice, and the new snow hid stretches of asphalt as slick as glass.

Her old station wagon needed better snow tires. The rear end slewed sickeningly as she turned onto Main Street and her stomach skidded with it, but there were no other vehicles on the road and she came through the turn without harm to anything but her nerves.

Only two cars were parked in the bank's lot, the aged maroon Lincoln she recognized as Dennison's and a big, shiny black SUV that looked as if it could climb Everest in a blizzard and come through laughing.

Dennison would have sent his employees home early because of the storm. The SUV probably belonged to some tourist on his way to ski country who'd stopped to use the ATM.

Tally parked and got out of the station wagon. The double doors to the bank opened as she reached them, revealing Walter Dennison wearing a black topcoat over his usual gray suit.

"You're late, Ms. Sommers."

He whispered the words. And shot a quick look over his shoulder. Tally felt a stab of panic. The black car. The paleness of Dennison's face. His whisper.

Was the bank being held up?

"I'm sorry," she said, trying to peer past him, "but the roads—"

"I understand." He hesitated. "Ms. Sommers. Tally. There's something you need to know."

Oh, God. It was true. She'd walked into a holdup in progress—

"I sold the bank."

She stared at him blankly. "What?"

"I said, I sold the bank."

He might as well have been speaking another language. Sold the bank? How could he have done that? The Dennison family had started the Shelby Bank in the early 1800s.

"I don't understand, Mr. Dennison. Why would you—"

"It's nothing for the town to worry about. The new owner will keep everything just as it is." Dennison cleared his throat. "Almost everything."

His eyes shifted from hers, and Tally's stomach dropped. There could only be one reason he'd wanted to see her.

"What about the new payment arrangements on my loan?"

She saw Dennison's adam's apple move up, then down. He opened his mouth as if he were going to speak. Instead, he shouldered past her, turned up his collar and went out into the storm. Tally stared after him as his lean figure was lost in a swirling maelstrom of white.

"Mr. Dennison! Wait!" Her voice rose. "Will this affect my loan? You said the new owner will keep everything just as it is—"

"Not quite everything," a familiar voice said.

And even as her heart pounded, as she swung toward the open bank doors and told herself it couldn't be true, she knew what she would see.

That voice could belong to only one man.

DANTE SMILED when Taylor turned toward him.

Her face was white with shock.

Excellent. He'd wanted her stunned by the sight of

him. Things were going precisely as he'd intended, despite how quickly he'd had to work. He'd put his plan in motion in less than a week, first convincing the old man to sell and then getting the authorities to approve the sale, but he was Dante Russo.

People always deferred to him.

This morning, he'd phoned Dennison and told him he'd be there at three. Told him, as well, to notify Taylor to be at the bank at four.

Promptly at four.

And, of course, not to mention anything about the bank's new ownership.

Dante's lips curved in a tight smile. He'd figured Taylor would be on edge to start with. A woman who'd put up her home as equity for a loan of $175,000.00 she couldn't pay would not be at ease. Add in Dennison's refusal to explain the reason for the meeting and the warning to be prompt, her nerves would be stretched to the breaking point.

His smile faded. The only thing that would have made this more interesting was if Samuel Gardner was with her, but from the investigator's comments, he'd gathered that his former mistress's new lover didn't stand up to life's tougher moments.

"Why didn't Sam Gardner sign for the loan?" he'd asked Dennison.

The old man had looked at him as if he were insane.

"Buying a bank on a seeming whim, suggesting something anyone in town would know is impossible... You have a strange sense of humor, Mr. Russo," he'd said with a thin-lipped Yankee smile.

Dante stood away from the door.

Dennison was wrong. There was nothing the least bit humorous about this situation. It was payback, pure and simple.

And it was time Taylor knew it.

"Aren't you going to come inside and face me, *cara?*" he said, his tone deliberately soft and coaxing. "Perhaps not. Facing me is not your forte, is it?"

He saw her stiffen. She probably wanted to run, but she didn't. Instead, she raised her chin, squared her shoulders and stepped inside the bank. He had to admire her courage, the way she was girding herself for confrontation.

She had no way of knowing that nothing she could do would be enough. The news he was going to give her was bad, and it delighted him to do it.

"Hello, Dante."

Her voice trembled. Her face had taken on some color, though it was still pale. Three years. Three years since he'd seen her...

And she was still beautiful.

More beautiful than his memory of her, if that were possible. Was it time that had made her mouth seem even softer, her eyes wider and darker?

Still, time had not been completely kind. It had affected her in other ways.

Purple shadows lay beneath her eyes. Her hair was pulled back in an unbecoming knot and he had the indefensible urge to close the distance between them, take out the pins and let all those lustrous cinnamon strands tumble free.

He let his gaze move over her slowly, from her face all the way to her feet and back again. A frown creased his forehead. He'd never seen her in anything but elegantly tailored clothing. Designer suits and gowns, spiked heels that could give a man dangerous fantasies, her face perfectly made up, her hair impeccably cut and styled.

Things were different now. The lapels of her coat were frayed. Her boots were the no-nonsense kind meant for rough weather. Her hair was in that ridiculous knot and her face was bare of everything but lipstick—lipstick and the shadows of exhaustion under her eyes.

He spoke without thinking. "What's happened to you?" he said sharply. "Have you been ill?"

"How nice of you to ask."

She was still pale but her gaze was steady and her words were brittle with sarcasm. He moved quickly; before she could step back he was a breath away, his hand wrapped around her arm.

"I asked you a question. Answer it."

A flush rose in her cheeks. "I'm not ill. I'm simply living in the real world. It's a place where people work hard for what they have. Where you can't just snap your fingers and expect everyone to leap to do your bidding, but then, what would you know of such things?"

What, indeed? It was none of her business, of anyone's business, that he'd started his life scrounging for money, that he'd worked his hands raw in construction jobs when he came to the States, or that he could still remember what it was like to go to sleep hungry.

He'd never snapped his fingers and never would, but he'd be damned if he'd explain that to anyone.

"And your lover? He permits this?"

She looked at him as if he'd lost his mind. "My what?"

"Another question you don't want to answer. That's all right. I have plenty of time."

Tally wrenched free of his grasp. "I'm the one with questions, Dante. What are you doing here?"

"We haven't seen each other in a long time, *cara*." A slow smile that turned her blood to ice eased across his lips. "Surely, we have other things to talk about first."

"We have nothing to talk about."

"But we do. You know that."

She didn't know anything. That was the problem. What did he know? Did he know about Sam? She didn't think so. Surely, he'd have tossed that at her already, if he did.

Then, what did he want? He wasn't here for a visit. He hadn't bought the Shelby bank on a whim…

The loan. Her loan. Oh God, oh God…

"Ah," he said slyly, "your face is an open book. Have you thought of some things we might wish to discuss?"

She couldn't let him see her fear. There had to be some way she could gain the upper hand.

"What I know," Tally said, "is that we never talked in the past. We went to dinner, to parties…" She took a steadying breath. "And we went to bed."

His mouth twisted. Had she struck a nerve?

"I'm glad you remember that."

"Is that why you came here, Dante? To remind me that we used to have sex together? Or to ask why I left you?" Somehow, she managed a chilly smile. "Really, I thought you'd understand. My note—"

"Your note was a bad joke."

Tally shrugged her shoulders. "It was honest. Or did it never occur to you that a woman is no different from a man? I mean, yes, we can pretend in ways a man can't, but sooner or later, things grow, well, old."

Dante's face contorted with anger. "You're a liar!"

"Come on, admit it. We'd been together for months. It was fun for a long time but then—"

She gasped as he caught hold of her and encircled her throat with his hand.

"I remember how you were in bed," he said, his voice a low growl. "Are you telling me it was all a performance?"

He tugged her closer, until her body brushed his and she had to tilt back her head to look into his eyes. It was deliberate, damn him, a way of emphasizing his strength, his size, his domination.

God, how she hated him! Three years, three endless years, and he was still furious because she'd walked out on him, but she'd done what she had to do to survive. To protect her secret from his unpredictable Sicilian ego.

"You were fire in my arms." His eyes, the color of smoke, locked on hers. She tried to look away but his hand was like a collar around her throat. When he urged her chin up, she had no choice but to meet his gaze. "You cried out as I came inside you. Your womb contracted around me. Would you have me believe you faked that, too?"

"Is it impossible for you to be a gentleman?" Tally said, hating herself for the way her voice shook.

His smile was slow and sexy and so dangerous it made her heartbeat quicken.

"But I was a gentleman with you. Was that a mistake? Perhaps you didn't want a gentleman in your bed." She gasped as he forced her head back. "Is that why you ran away in the middle of the night?"

"I left you, period. Don't make it sound so dramatic."

"Left me for what, exactly? The glory of an existence in the middle of nowhere? A bank account with nothing in it?" His tone turned silken. "I think not, *cara*. I think you left me for a new lover who isn't a gentleman at all."

"I don't know what you're talking about!"

He thrust his fingers into her hair. The pins that held it confined clattered sharply against the marble floor as the strands of gold-burnished cinnamon came loose and fell over her shoulders.

"Is that it? Was I too gentle with you?" He wound her hair around his fist and lowered his head until his face was an inch from hers. "Had you hoped I would do things to you, demand things of you, that people only whisper about?"

"Dante. This is— It's crazy. I don't— I didn't…" She swallowed dryly. "Let me go."

She'd meant the words to be a command. Instead, they were a whisper. He smiled with amusement, and she felt an electric jolt in her blood.

"I said, let go… Or did you come here thinking you could bully me back into your arms?"

His eyes grew dark; she saw his mouth twist. The seconds ticked away and then, when her heart seemed ready to leap from her breast, he thrust her from him, stepped back and folded his arms.

"Never that," he said coolly. "And you're right. Things were over between us. I knew it. In fact, that was the reason I went to see you that night. I wanted to tell you we were finished." He gave a quick smile. "As you say, *cara,* things get old."

She'd known the truth but hearing it made it worse.

Still, she showed no reaction. He wanted her to squirm, and she'd be damned if she would.

"Is that what this is about? That the great Dante Russo wants to be sure I understand I made the first move only because your timing was off?"

Dante chuckled. "Bright as always, Taylor—though you surely don't believe I bought this bank and made this trip only so I could tell you it was pure luck you ended our affair before I did."

Tally moistened her lips with the tip of her tongue. She was dying inside, but she'd be damned if she'd let him know it.

"No. I'm not that naive. You bought the bank because—" Desperately, she ran through the terms of the loan in her mind. Could he do that? Could he cancel what Dennison had already approved? "Because you think you can cancel my loan."

"Think?" he said, very softly. "You underestimate me. I can do whatever I wish, but canceling a loan that already exists would take more time and effort than it's worth." He smiled. "So I'm going to do the next best thing. I'm reinstating the original repayment terms."

Her gaze flew to his. "Reinstating them?" she said stupidly. "I don't understand."

"It's simple, *cara*," he said, almost gently. "As of now, you will pay the amount you are supposed to pay each month."

Tally thought of the four-figure number the loan called for. She was paying a quarter of that amount now, and barely managing it.

"That's—it's out of the question. I can't possibly—"

"Additionally, you will pay the amount that's in arrears." He took a slip of paper from his pocket and held it out toward her. His lips curved. "Plus interest, of course."

Tally looked at the number on the paper and laughed. It was either that or weep.

"I don't have that kind of money!"

"Ah." Dante sighed. "I thought not. In that case, you leave me no choice but to start foreclosure proceedings against your home."

She felt the blood drain from her face. "Foreclosure proceedings?"

"This was a home equity loan. You put up your house as collateral." Another quick, icy smile. "If you don't understand what that means, perhaps your lover can explain it to you."

"Are you crazy?" Tally's voice rose. "You can't do this! You can't take my house. You can't!" Her hands came up like a fighter's, fists at the ready as if she would beat him into understanding the horror of his plan. "Damn you, there are rules!"

"You've forgotten what you know about me," Dante said coldly. "I make my own rules."

He proved it by gathering her into his arms and kissing her.

CHAPTER THREE

HE WAS KISSING HER, Dante told himself, because she'd lied to him a few minutes ago.

Why else would he want her in his arms, except to make her confess to the lie?

Taylor had never faked her responses in bed, and he'd be damned if he'd let her pretend she had.

He was over her, but she knew just the right buttons to push. Well, so did he. He'd kiss her until she melted against him the way she used to and then he'd step back and say, *You see, Taylor? That's the price liars pay.*

Which was why he was kissing her.

Or trying to.

The problem was that he had cornered a wildcat. She fought back, twisted her head to the side to avoid his mouth and pummeled his shoulders with her fists.

When none of that worked, she sank her teeth in his ear lobe so hard he hissed with pain.

"Damn you, woman!"

"Let go of me, you—you—"

Her fist flew by his jaw. Grimly, Dante snared both her hands in one of his and pinned them to his chest. Her knee came up but he felt it happening and yanked her hard against him to immobilize her. She was helpless now, pinned between him and the wall beside the double doors.

"Take your hands off me, Russo! If you don't, so help me—"

"So help you, what? What will you do? How will you stop me from proving what a little liar you are?"

"I don't know what you're talking about. I am not a—"

He bent his head and captured her mouth with his. She nipped his lip, her teeth sharp as a cat's. He tasted blood but if she thought that would stop him, she didn't know him very well.

He would win this battle.

He had the right to know why she'd lied about what she'd felt when he made love to her. And to know why she'd left him.

He wanted answers and, damn it, he was going to get them.

He caught her face in his hands. Kissed her again, angling his mouth over hers, penetrating her with his tongue. He remembered how she'd loved it when he kissed her this way. Deep. Wet. Hot. He'd loved kisses like this, too...

He still did.

Dio, the feel of her in his arms. Her breasts, soft against his chest. Her hips, cradling his erection.

He wanted her, and it had nothing to do with anger.

It was the feel of her. The taste. The scent of her skin. He remembered all of it, everything making love to her had done to them both, and his kiss gentled, his touch turned from demand to caress, and a little sigh whispered from her lips to his.

She was trembling, but not with fear.

It was with desire. For this. For him.

Something began to unlock inside him. Something so primitive he couldn't put a name to it. He only knew that the woman in his arms still belonged to him.

He swept his hands into her hair. All that lush, cinnamon-hued silk tumbled over his fingers.

"Tell me you want me," he said, his voice rough and thick.

She shook her head in denial. "No," she whispered.

But her eyes were pools of darkness as she looked up at him, as her hands spread over his chest.

"I don't," she said, "I don't…"

He took her mouth again and suddenly she gave the wild little cry he had heard her make a thousand times in the past. It excited him as much now as it had then, and when she rose on her toes and wound her arms around his neck, whispered "Dante," as if he were the only man in the world who could ever make her feel this way, he went crazy with desire.

It had been so long. Oh, so long since he'd possessed her. He was on fire…and so was she.

Saying her name, blind to everything but passion, Dante fumbled with the buttons of her coat. When they didn't come undone quickly enough, he cursed and tore the coat open.

He had to cup her breasts or he would die. Had to thrust his knee between her thighs and hear her cry out again as she moved against him. Had to shove up her skirt, slip his hand between her thighs and, yes oh yes, feel her heat, yes, feel the wetness of her desire, yes, yes…

Her head fell back like a flower on a wind-bent stalk.

She whispered his name over and over, knotted her fingers in his hair as she lifted herself to him.

Blindly, he lifted her off her feet. Spread her thighs. Reached for his zipper. Now. Right now. He would be inside her. Lost in her silken folds…

"Mr. Dennison? I didn't finish cleanin' but considerin' the storm's turnin' into a blizzard, an'… Whoa!"

The thin, shocked voice had all the power of an explosion.

Dante whirled around, automatically shielding Taylor with his body. A grizzled old man in overalls and work boots stood next to the tellers' cages, his eyes wide and his jaw somewhere down around his ankles.

"Who," Dante said coldly, "are you?"

Tally pulled the lapels of her coat together and peered past Dante's shoulder, heart thumping in her ears.

"It's Esau Staunton. The janitor," she whispered in a shaky voice.

The old man was also Shelby's biggest gossip. By tomorrow, the whole town would know what had happened here this afternoon. She gave a soft moan of despair, and Dante put his arm around her and drew her forward so that she was pressed against his side. She stiffened and would have moved away but he spread his hand over her hip, the pressure of it insistent.

Was he trying to brand her? Or was he telling her this wasn't finished? Either way, she had to let him do it. Her legs had turned to jelly.

"Is that your name?" Dante said pleasantly. "Staunton?"

The old man swallowed audibly. "That's me." His

eyes danced to Taylor, then back to Dante. "Where's Mr. Dennison?"

"Mr. Dennison no longer owns this bank. I do. And you're right, Mr. Staunton. You should leave now, before the storm gets worse."

"You sure?" Again, the rheumy gaze fell on Taylor. "My boy's just pulled up at the curb in that red pickup, but, ah, if you or the lady wants—"

"Go home, Mr. Staunton," Dante said, his tone still pleasant but now backed with steel.

"Oh. Sure. Sure, I'll do that. Mr., ah, Mr.—"

"Russo. And there's one last thing." Dante spoke softly, in that same polite but unyielding voice. "I'm sure you understand that Ms. Sommers wouldn't want anyone to know about her fainting spell."

"Her fainting—"

"Surely, I can trust you to be discreet. People who work for me always are. And you do want to work for me, Esau, don't you?"

Another audible swallow. "Yessir. I do."

"Excellent. In that case, have a pleasant weekend."

The old man nodded and opened the double doors. The wind filled the room with its icy breath as he scrambled into the red pickup, which disappeared into the swirling snow.

"The old man was right," Dante said. "The storm's turned into a blizzard."

Tally stared at him. How could he talk about the weather after what he'd just done? Forcing his kisses on her. His caresses. If the janitor hadn't turned up, who knew what would have happened?

As for his admonitions to the old man—did he really

think they meant anything here? By tomorrow, this sordid little story would be everywhere.

Not that it mattered.

Without a house, without an income, she and Sam wouldn't be living in Shelby much longer.

"Nothing to say, *cara?*"

She wrenched free of his encircling arm. "You've done what you came to do, Dante. More, thanks to…to that performance just now."

His eyebrows rose. "Is that what you call it?"

Amusement tinged the words. Oh, how she wanted to slap that smug, masculine smile from his face.

"You are—you are despicable. Do you understand? You are the most despicable, contemptible—"

The world blurred. She raised her hand and swung it, but his fingers curled around her wrist.

"Such a temper, *bellissima.* And all because I caught you in a lie." His smile vanished. "You wanted me three years ago and you want me now."

"If you ever come near me again—"

"Don't make threats, Taylor. Not unless you're prepared to back them up."

She wanted to scream. To weep. To lunge at him again—but none of that would change anything. Because of him, her life had almost come apart before. Now, it lay in tatters at her feet.

The only thing left was a dignified retreat.

"You're right," she said, forcing herself to sound calm. "No threats. Just a promise. I don't ever want to see you again. If you come after me, I'll go to court and charge you with harassment. Is that clear?"

He laughed. And, before he could stop her a second time, Tally slapped his face.

Fury darkened his eyes. He reached for her, a harsh Sicilian oath spilling from his lips, but she slipped by him, yanked the doors open and ran.

She heard him shout her name but she didn't look back. The parking lot was a sea of white; the wind tore at her with icy talons as she fought her way to her station wagon, pulled the door open, got behind the wheel and slammed down the lock.

Just in time. A second later, Dante grabbed the door handle, then banged his fist against the window.

"Taylor! Open this door."

Her hands were shaking. It took two tries before she could jab the key into the ignition. The engine coughed, coughed again—and died.

A sob burst from her throat. "Come on," she said, turning the key, "come on, damn it. Start!"

"Taylor!" Another blow against the window. "What in hell do you think you're doing?"

Getting away. That was what she was doing. Dante had destroyed everything she'd built over the last years. He'd taken her home with a stroke of the pen, her pride with a kiss she hadn't wanted, her reputation with an X-rated scene she didn't want to think about.

And all he'd proved was what they'd both already known, that he was powerful and brutal, that he had no heart. That he could still make her respond to him, make her forget what he was and drown in his kisses....

"Taylor!"

She turned the key again. Not even a cough this time. *Calm down,* she told herself. Take it easy. The engine needed work, she knew that, but it had gotten her here, hadn't it?

The car wouldn't start because of the cold, that was all. Or maybe she'd flooded it. You could fit what she knew about cars inside a thimble and have room for the rest of the sewing kit, but wasn't there something about not giving a cold engine too much—

The station wagon rocked under the force of Dante's fist.

"Damn you, woman, are you out of your mind? Get out of that car! You can't drive in a blizzard."

She couldn't stay here, either. Not with him. And there was Sam to worry about. Was Sam safe at the Millers'? Yes. Of course. Sheryl and Dan were Sam's friends as well as hers. Still, she'd worry until she reached home.

If there was one thing life had taught her, it was that anything was possible.

One last try. Turn the key. Touch the gas pedal lightly…

Nothing. Nothing! Tally screamed in frustration and pounded the heels of her hands against the steering wheel.

"Listen to me," Dante said, calmly now, as if he were trying to talk sense to a child.

How could she not listen? They were inches apart, separated only by glass.

"Come back inside until the storm is over. I won't touch you. I swear it."

She almost laughed. What could he possibly know of a New England winter? The storm might last for days. Days, alone with him? With a man who'd just promised not to touch her in a way that made it clear he was sure she was helpless against him?

"Taylor. Be reasonable. We'll phone for help. This town has snowplows, doesn't it?"

Of course it did. But would the phones work? The first thing that always failed in bad weather were the telephone lines.

"Damn you, woman," Dante roared. "Can't you be without your lover for a few hours? Would you risk your neck, just to get back to him?"

So much for logic and reason.

Dante cursed, yanked at the door and it flew open. Tally grabbed for the handle but he was already leaning into the car, gathering her into his arms and striding to the bank through the blinding snow, head bent against the shrieking wind.

When they reached the entrance, he put her down.

"Just stand still," he said grimly. "Once we're inside, I'll call the police. For all I give a damn, you can lock yourself in the vault until they arrive."

He reached for the brass handle and pulled.

Nothing happened.

He grunted, wrapped both hands around the handle and pulled harder. But the doors were locked.

He spat out a word in Sicilian. Tally didn't need a translator to know what it meant. Here was one situation he couldn't control. Neither could she. The doors were probably on a timer. They wouldn't open until Monday.

People died in storms like this, and she knew it.

So, evidently, did Dante.

He picked her up again. She didn't fight him this time. The footing was slippery; he stumbled, recovered his balance and she automatically wrapped her arms around his neck. Snow crunched underfoot as he made his way toward the black SUV she knew must be his. Halfway there, he dug his keys from his pocket, pointed the remote at the vehicle and unlocked it.

He put her in the passenger seat, hurried to the driver's side and got in. For a long moment, they sat without looking at each other. Then he took a cell phone from his pocket and flipped it open.

"It won't work," Tally said wearily, leaning back in her seat.

Dante turned toward her. Her face was pale. He sensed that her anger had given way to resignation. It was an emotion neither of them could afford in a situation like this.

"Well, then," he said briskly, "we'll just have to come up with another plan."

He turned the ignition key so that he could read the instrument panel. The gas gauge, in particular, though he knew what he'd find. He'd been in such a damned rush to get to the bank before Taylor arrived…

One look confirmed what he'd suspected.

"We don't have much gas. Just enough to run the engine for maybe twenty, thirty minutes. After that—" *After that, they'd freeze.* "So," he said, again in that brisk tone, "here's what we're going to do. I'll go for help. You stay here and turn on the engine every ten minutes. Let the car warm up, then shut if off. Do that as long as you can and I'll do my best to find help quickly."

"Don't be a fool! You won't get a hundred yards."

"Why, *cara*," he said, the words laced with sarcasm, "I didn't think you cared."

She didn't. But she did care about Sam. A moment ago, she'd almost let despair overtake her. Now she knew she couldn't let that happen. She had to live. To live for Sam.

There was only one choice. It was a risk in endless ways, but staying here was worse.

She took a deep breath. "Are you a good driver?"

"Of course."

Such macho intensity! Any other time, she'd have laughed.

"And is there enough gas in the tank to go fifteen miles?"

He nodded. "Just about."

"Then start the car. I'll get us to my house. My neighbor has a truck and snowplow. He can lead you to a place near the highway—tow you, if necessary— where there's a gas station and a motel. You'll be fine there until the storm's over."

"And you? Will you be fine, as well?"

Tally looked at Dante. His eyes were cool, making it clear his was a polite question and nothing more.

"I'm not your concern," she said. "I never was."

A muscle knotted in his jaw. Then he nodded, turned the engine on and headed out of the parking lot and into the teeth of the storm.

THE WORLD HAD TURNED into an undulating sea of white. Shifts in the wind's direction revealed only an occasional landmark, but that was enough.

The heavy vehicle, Dante's skill at the wheel and Tally's knowledge of the roads combined to get them safely to her driveway.

They battled their way to the door. Tally dug out her keys; Dante automatically reached for them as he used to when he saw her home in New York, and they waged a silent, brief struggle until he held up his hands in surrender and let her unlock the door herself.

She paused in the doorway.

The danger of the drive here had deprived her of rational thought. Now she was making up for it with frantic desperation. Were any of Sam's things in the kitchen? She didn't think so. Besides, it was too late to worry about it now.

If there were, she'd come up with some kind of explanation. In the last hour, she'd learned to be an accomplished liar.

She stepped into the room, fingers mentally crossed, with Dante close behind her, and reached for the light switch. The room remained dark. The power was out, as she'd figured it would be. The phone, too. All she heard when she picked up the handset was silence.

"It would seem you're stuck with a guest," Dante said coolly.

Tally didn't answer. She felt her way to the cupboard and took out the candles and matches she kept handy for just such occasions. When the candles were lit, she put one on the sink and another on the round wooden table near the window.

A shudder raced through her. The kitchen was the smallest room in the house but an hour or two without the furnace going had turned it into a walk-in refrigerator.

"Are you cold?"

"I'm fine."

Dante frowned, shrugged off his leather jacket and

draped it around her shoulders. "You'll never be a good liar, *cara*."

"I don't need—"

"You damned well do! Keep the jacket until the room warms up." He jerked his chin at the old stone fireplace that took up most of one long wall. "Is that real?"

"Of course it's real," Tally said brusquely, trying not inhale the scents of night and leather and man that enveloped her. "This is New England, not Manhattan. Nobody here has time for pretense."

A smile twisted across his mouth. "What an interesting observation," he said softly, "all things considered."

She felt her face heat. "I didn't mean—"

"No. I'm sure you didn't." He held out his hand. "Give me those matches and I'll make a fire."

"That's not necessary."

"Nothing is necessary," he said curtly. "Not if it involves me, is that correct?"

He'd come so close to the truth that she was afraid to meet his eyes, but that had been their initial agreement, hadn't it? Their relationship had been based on accommodation, not necessity. No strings. No commitment. No leaning on him for anything...

"Look, I know you want me gone," he said impatiently, "and believe me, I'll be happy to comply, but until then I'll be damned if I'm going to freeze just so you can prove a point. Give me the matches."

He was right, even if she hated to admit it. She tossed him the matches and watched as he knelt before her grandmother's old brick hearth and built a fire. Just seeing the orange flames made her feel better and she moved closer to them, hands outstretched so she could catch some of their warmth.

"Better?"

Tally nodded. All she could do now was wait for the storm's power to abate. At least she wasn't worried about Sam anymore. She'd seen the Millers' lights glowing when they drove past their house. She'd forgotten that Dan and Sheryl had a generator. Their place would be snug. Sam would have a hot meal, a warm bed...

"So. You inherited this from your grandmother?"

Her gaze shot to Dante. Arms folded, face unreadable, he was looking around the kitchen as if it were an alien planet. It probably was, to a man accustomed to luxury.

"Yes," she replied coldly. "And now I'm about to lose it to you."

"And where is your lover? Out of town? Or in another room, afraid to face me?"

"I told you, I don't have a lover. And if I did, why would he fear you? My life is my own, Dante. You have no part in it."

"You made that clear the night you ran away."

"For God's sake, are we going to talk about that again?" Tally marched to the stove, filled a kettle with water, took it to the hearth and knelt down, searching for the best place to put it. "I left you. I was absolutely free to do that. I know it's hard to face, but I didn't need your permission."

"Common courtesy demanded more than that note."

"I don't think so."

"Damn it," he growled, clasping her shoulders and

drawing her up beside him, "I'm tired of you dancing away from my questions. I want to know the reason you left."

"I told you. Our affair was over." She looked straight into his eyes. "And we both knew it."

She was right...wasn't she? Hadn't he come to the same conclusion? That it was time to end things? Not that it mattered. He *hadn't* ended the relationship. She had.

Wasn't that the reason he was here? Except, she was doing it again. Taking the upper hand, and he didn't like it.

"I never gave you the right to speak for me," he said sharply.

"No. You didn't. So I'll speak for myself." She took a deep breath and turned away. "I wanted a change."

Dante's mouth thinned. "You mean, you became involved with another man."

"That's ridiculous! I didn't—"

She cried out as he caught her and swung her toward him. "More lies," he growled.

"For the last time, there is no other man!"

"There is. I know his name." His hands dug into her flesh. "Now I want to know if you respond to him as you did to me a little while ago."

"Respond?" She gave a harsh laugh. "Is that what you call it? You—you forced yourself on me!"

It was a foolish thing to say. His nostrils flared like a stallion's at the scent of a mare in heat.

"You don't learn, do you?" he said softly. "You keep making statements and I end up having to prove that they're lies."

Tally looked up into the face of the man who had once been the center of her universe. How could she have forgotten how beautiful he was? And how cruel?

"We're both adults, *cara*. Why not admit we want each other?"

"Didn't you just say you knew I was eager to see you gone? That you'd be happy to go?" Damn it, why did she sound breathless? "Didn't you say that?"

He didn't answer. Instead, he cupped her face and lifted it to his. "Kiss me once," he whispered. "Just once. Then, if you don't want to make love, I promise, I won't touch you again."

"I don't have to kiss you to know the—"

His mouth took hers captive. Tally made a little sound of protest. Then his arms went around her and she let him gather her into his embrace, let his lips part hers and she knew nothing had changed, not when it came to this. To wanting his touch. His mouth. His body, hardening against hers...

The door flew open; the gust of wind that followed slammed it, hard, against the wall as a small woman cradling a grocery bag in one arm all but sailed into the kitchen.

"Sorry not to knock," Sheryl Miller said breathlessly, "but I don't have a free hand. I brought you leftovers from dinner and a loaf of oatmeal bread I baked this morning. Dan's going to get his mom and I said I'd go with—" Her mouth formed a perfect circle as she peered around the bag. "Oh! Oh, I'm sorry, Tally. I didn't know you had company."

Neither Tally or Dante answered. Both of them were staring at the toddler, round as a snowman in a raspberry-pink snowsuit, who clung to Sheryl's free hand.

"Hi, Mama," Samantha Gardner Sommers said happily, and flew to her mother's arms.

CHAPTER FOUR

FOR A MOMENT, no one moved but the child.

Then, as if someone had pushed a button, the room came to life again. The woman in the doorway, her face a polite mask, put the bag she'd been holding on the counter. Taylor scooped the toddler into her arms, and Dante...

Dante forced himself to breathe.

Mama? Was that really what the child had said? Taylor was staring at him over the little girl's head. Her face had gone white. So, he suspected, had his.

"Who is this?" he said hoarsely.

The woman glanced at Taylor. Then she took a step forward. "I'm Sheryl Miller. Tally's neighbor."

His head swung toward the woman. He thought of saying he didn't mean her, that he didn't give a damn who she was, but that would have been stupid. He needed time to get hold of himself and she had given him exactly that.

Oh yes, he needed time because what he was thinking was surely impossible.

"And you are?" Sheryl said, breaking the strained silence.

"Dante Russo." Dante forced a polite smile. "Taylor and I—"

"We knew each other in New York," Tally said quickly. A little color had returned to her face but it only made her look feverish. "He was in the area and—and he thought he'd drop by."

A horn beeped outside. The Miller woman ignored it. "Funny," she said, "but Tally never mentioned you."

He wanted to tell the woman to get out. To leave him alone so he could ask Taylor who this child was, why she'd called her Mama, but he knew better than to push things. The tension in the room was thick. Taylor's neighbor was already looking at him as if he might be a serial killer.

"No," he said politely, smiling through his teeth, "I'm sure she didn't."

The woman ignored him. "Tally? Is everything okay?"

Tally swallowed a wave of hysterical laughter. Nothing was okay. Nothing would ever be okay again unless she could come up with a story to change the way Dante was looking at her and Sam.

"You want me to tell Dan to come in?"

"No! Oh, no, Sheryl. I mean—" What *did* she mean? "It's as I said. Dante is an old—an old—"

"Friend," Dante said, his tone level. "I thought I'd stop by and see how Taylor was adjusting to small-town life."

The Miller woman looked doubtful but Tally said yes, that was it, and smiled, and finally the woman smiled, too.

"Why wouldn't she adjust? Didn't she ever tell you she's a small-town girl at heart? That she comes from Shelby?"

"No. But then, I'm starting to realize there are lots

of things she didn't tell me." Dante looked at Taylor. "Isn't that right, *cara?*"

Taylor didn't answer. That was good because it meant she knew that whatever she said now would only fuel the fury building inside him.

The horn beeped again. "Dan wants to get going," Sheryl said. She peeled off a glove and offered Dante a brisk handshake. "Nice to have met you." She leaned forward, as if to share a confidence. "Tally can use the company. I keep telling her she needs to get out more but what with Sam, well, you know how it is."

"No," Dante said, forcing another smile, "I'm afraid I don't."

Sheryl grinned. "Men never do. Anyway, it's good to see someone from her old life drop by."

"That's definitely what I am. Someone from Taylor's old life."

This time, the horn beeped three times.

"Okay, okay," Sheryl muttered, "I'm coming. Tally? I was going to say, if you want to come with us, I'm sure Dan's mother wouldn't mind."

For a wild moment, Tally imagined running out into the storm with Sam, getting into the truck, telling Dan to drive and drive and drive until she'd put a million miles between Dante and her—

"Tally?"

What was that old saying? You could run, but you couldn't hide.

"Thanks," she said brightly, "but we'll be fine."

The Miller woman looked unconvinced. Dante put his arm around Tally. When she stiffened, he dug his fingers into her flesh in mute warning.

"Taylor's right. We'll be fine." He drew his lips back from his teeth and hoped the result would still approximate a smile. "The snow, a fire, candlelight...it's quite romantic, especially for old friends. Isn't that right, *cara?*"

The child, thumb tucked in her mouth, looked at him. *Liar,* her round green eyes seemed to say. But the woman's big smile assured him she'd bought the story.

"In that case, I'm off. It was nice meeting you, Mr. Russo."

Dante held his smile until the door closed. *Now,* he told himself, and dropped his arm from Taylor's shoulders.

"Whose child is this?"

No preliminaries, she thought dizzily. No safe answers, either.

"Taylor. I asked you a question. Is the child yours?"

Sam chose that moment to give a huge yawn. Tally grabbed at the diversion.

"Somebody's sleepy," she said, ignoring Dante and the pounding of her heart.

"Am not," Sam said, yawning again.

Despite herself, Tally smiled. "Are, too," she said gently. She buried her face in her daughter's sweet-smelling neck as she carried her to the small sofa near the fireplace and sat her down. She tugged off the baby's boots, zipped her out of her snowsuit but left on the warm sweater and tights beneath it.

"How about taking a nap, sweetie? Right here, by the fire. Would you like that?"

"Wan' Teddy."

"Teddy! Of course. I'll get him. You just put your head down and I'll get Teddy and your yellow blankey, okay?"

"'Kay," Sam said, eyelids already drooping.

Tally rose to her feet and forced herself to look at Dante. "Don't," she began to say, but caught herself in time. Don't what? Go near my child? That wasn't the problem. The questions that blazed in his silver eyes was the problem.

So was answering them.

By the time she returned, Samantha was fast asleep. Tally covered her, tucked the teddy bear beside her, smoothed back the baby's hair…

"Stop playing for time."

She swung around. Dante, standing only inches away, might have been carved from granite. Her heart was beating in her throat but the biggest mistake she could make now would be to show her panic.

"Please keep your voice down. I don't want you to wake Sam."

"Sam?" His mouth twisted. "The child's name. Not your lover's. Why did you let me think otherwise?"

She busied herself picking up the boots and snowsuit from the floor.

"I had no idea what you thought. Besides, why would I care? This is my life. I don't owe you explan—"

She gasped as his hand closed, hard, on her wrist. "No games," he said in a soft, dangerous voice. "I warn you, I'm not in the mood."

"And I'm not in the mood for being bullied. Take your hand off me."

Their eyes met and held. Slowly, he released her. Tally took a last look at her sleeping daughter, then walked briskly into the kitchen with Dante on her heels.

"I'm still waiting for an answer. Is the child yours?"

The million-dollar question. It wasn't as if she hadn't envisioned this scene before and all the possible ways to handle it. Dante would demand to know whose baby this was and she'd come up with a creative reply.

She'd say she was raising the child of a sister or a dear friend. Or she'd tell him that she'd adopted Sam. Any of those explanations had seemed plausible, but now, with his cold eyes boring into hers, Tally knew she'd been kidding herself.

A man with Dante's resources would prove she was lying in the blink of an eye.

"It's a simple question, Taylor. Is the child yours?"

In the end, there was only one possible response. She gave it on a forced exhalation of breath.

"Yes. She's mine."

She steadied herself for what would come next. Anger that she hadn't told him he'd made her pregnant? A demand to claim that which was his? Or perhaps, by some miracle, a thawing of his ice-clad heart at the realization he had a daughter.

Later, she'd weep bitter tears at the memory of those possibilities and how reasonable they'd seemed.

"So, that's the reason you left me. Because you were pregnant."

She nodded and searched his face for some hint of what he was thinking.

"Answer the question! Was your pregnancy the reason you ran away?"

"I didn't run away."

His mouth thinned. "No. Of course you didn't."

"I'm sure you think I should have told you, but—"

"You were quite right, keeping the information to yourself," he said coldly. "However you imagined I'd react, the reality would have been worse."

Tears blurred her eyes. "Yes," she said. "I know that now."

Dante caught her by the shoulders, his hands as hard as his eyes.

"I made myself clear from the start."

She couldn't help it. The tears she'd tried to control trembled on her lashes, then fell. She pulled free of his hands, went to the sink and made a pretense of straightening things that didn't need straightening.

"I know. That's why I didn't—"

"You were my mistress."

That dried her tears in a hurry. "I was never that."

"Don't mince words, damn it!" He came up behind her and swung her toward him. "You belonged to me."

"This jacket belongs to you," she said, shrugging it from her shoulders so it dropped to the floor. "And that vehicle in the driveway." Tally thumped her fist against her chest. "*I* am not property. I never belonged to you."

"No." His smile was as thin as a rapier. "As it turns out, you didn't." His grasp on her tightened. "I knew things had changed between us. I just didn't know the reason."

"I left you. Final answer."

"I thought it was that our relationship was growing old."

Amazing, that such cruel words could wound after all this time, but she'd sooner have died than let him know it.

"You're right. It was. It had. That's why—"

"Now I find out it wasn't that at all." He caught her face, lifted it to him so that their eyes met. "It was this," he said, jerking his chin toward the next room, where the baby lay sleeping. "You had a secret and you were so intent on keeping it from me that you kept yourself from me, too."

"Maybe you're not as thick-headed as you seem," Tally countered, trying for sarcasm and failing, if the twist of his lips was any indication.

"I could kill you," he said softly.

As if to prove it, one cool hand circled her throat. His touch was light, but she felt its warning pressure.

"Let go of me, Dante."

"There's not a court in the land that would convict me."

"This is America. Not Sicily." Tally put her hand over his. "Damn you, do you think I planned to get pregnant?"

He stared at her for a long minute. Then he dropped his hand to his side.

"No," he said. "I suppose not."

He strode away from her, his back rigid, and paced her kitchen like a caged lion.

Her heart thudded.

What was going on in his head? Would he turn his back and walk away? Or would his pride, whatever it was that drove him, demand that he stake his claim to her daughter? She'd do anything to avoid that, anything to keep this heartless man from being involved in raising Samantha.

"Dante." Tally hesitated. "I know you're angry but— but you must believe me. I did what I thought was—"

"You told me you were using a diaphragm."

"Yes. I know. But—"

He swung toward her. "But not with him."

Tally blinked. "What?"

"I want to know who he is."

"You want—you want to know—"

"The name of your child's father. The man you took as a lover while you still belonged to me."

She stared at him in disbelief. He wasn't angry because she'd left him without telling him she was carrying his baby. He was angry because he thought she'd cheated on him.

Was that how little he thought of her? That she'd betrayed him while they were lovers? God oh God, she wanted to launch herself at him. Claw his heart out, except he had no heart.

But then, she'd always known that. It was what had made her weep at night toward the end.

She'd never so much as looked at anyone else while they'd been together. She'd never looked at anyone in the years since, either, because she was a fool, a fool, a fool…

"I am assuming," he said, "that you are not going to tell me I sired this child."

Sired Sam? He made it sound like a procedure performed in a veterinarian's office…but that was fine. Every word he said assured her she'd been right to leave him when she did.

"Damn you," he snarled, catching her by the shoulders, "answer me!"

She could do that. She could do whatever it took, to get this man out of her life.

"You can relax, Dante. I promise you, I'm not going to tell you that you are Samantha's father. If you want that in writing, I'll be happy to oblige."

A muscle bunched in his jaw. "You still haven't said who he was, this man who took you to his bed while you were still sleeping in mine."

Tally wrenched free. "You have it wrong. It was you who slept in *my* bed, remember?"

"Answer me, damn it. Who is he?"

"That's none of your business."

"I told you, you belonged to me. That makes it my business."

"And *I* told *you,* I am not property!" She looked up at him, hating him for what he was, for what he thought, for what she'd once felt in his arms. "What's the matter? Have I wounded your pride? Will I wound it even more if I tell you I was only with him once? That's all it took for him to give me his child."

He grabbed her, his face so white, eyes so hot, that she thought she'd finally pushed him too far, but that didn't matter. She'd wanted to hurt him enough to draw blood and she had...

With the truth.

She knew exactly when their child—when *her* child—had been conceived. On the night of his birthday. She'd learned the date by accident, when he left his wallet open on the nightstand with his driver's license in view. She'd made dinner, baked a cake, bought him a present because she'd—because she'd wanted to.

After, Dante had made such tender love to her that she'd looked into her own heart and come as close as she'd dared to admitting what she felt for him.

"Stay with me tonight," she'd whispered, as they lay in each other's arms.

He hadn't.

After he was gone, she'd felt more alone than she'd ever thought possible. Not just alone but abandoned. Used, not by his heart but by his body.

She'd cried softly as night faded to morning. Hours later, when she got up to shower, she'd discovered that her diaphragm had a pinpoint hole in it. She'd told herself it was nothing. It was her so-called safe time of the month and besides, what were the odds on becoming pregnant after just one night of unprotected sex?

Six weeks later, a home pregnancy kit proved that the odds were excellent.

Tally had considered the life she'd planned. A career, not for her ego but for security. Money in the bank that would guarantee she'd never have to depend on a man the way her mother had.

She'd visited her doctor. Asked tough questions, made tough decisions. And reversed herself on the subway ride home when she saw a young woman with a baby in her arms, the mother cooing, the baby laughing with unrestricted joy.

Her future had changed in that single instant.

Now, it was changing again. If she'd had any last, lingering doubts about her feelings for the man she'd once come close to thinking she loved, they were gone.

She looked pointedly at Dante's hand, encircling her wrist, then at his face.

"I want you out of here," she said softly. "Right now."

He looked at her for a long moment. Then, slowly and deliberately, he took his hand from her.

"I thought I knew you," he said in a low voice.

She almost laughed at the absurdity of those words. "You never knew me," she said.

"No. I didn't. I see that now." He plucked his leather jacket from where she'd dropped it and slipped it on. "Get yourself an attorney. A good one, because I'm going to start foreclosure proceedings as soon as I return to New York."

Panic took an oily slide in her belly. "I can make the payments on the loan. I *have* made them! All you have to do is check the bank records."

"The amount you've been paying each month is a joke. It has nothing to do with the loan agreement."

"But Walter Dennison said—"

"You're not dealing with Dennison. You're dealing with me."

She watched, transfixed, as he strolled to the door. At the last second, she went after him.

"Wait! Please, you can't… My daughter, Dante. My little girl. Surely you wouldn't punish an innocent child for my mistakes. That's not possible!"

"Anything is possible," he said coldly. "You proved that when you took a lover."

"Dante. Don't make me beg. Don't—"

"Why not?" He turned and clasped her elbows, lifting her to him until his empty eyes were all she could see. "I'd love to hear you beg, *cara*. It would fill my heart with joy."

The bitter tears she'd fought to suppress streamed down her cheeks.

"I hate you, Dante Russo. Hate you. Hate you. Hate—"

He took her mouth in a hard, deep kiss, one that demanded acquiescence. Tally fought it. Fought him as he cupped her face, held her prisoner to his plundering mouth until she knew she would kill him when he turned her free, kill him…

And then, slowly, his kiss changed. His lips softened

on hers. His tongue teased. His hands slid into her hair and she felt it again, after all these years, all this anguish and pain. The slow, dangerous heat low in her belly. The thickening of her blood. The need for him, only him…

Dante pushed her away.

"You belonged to me," he said roughly. "Only to me. I could have you again if I wished." His mouth twisted. "But why would I want another man's leavings?"

Then he put up his collar, opened the door and strode into the teeth of the storm.

CHAPTER FIVE

HOW MANY TIMES could a man be subjected to the saccharine nonsense of Christmas before he lost what remained of his sanity?

The holiday was still three weeks away and Dante was already tired of the music pouring out of shops and car radios. He'd seen enough artificial evergreens to last a lifetime, and he was damned close to telling the next sidewalk Santa exactly what he could do with his cheery ho-ho-ho.

New York, his city, belonged to tourists from Thanksgiving through the New Year. They descended on the Big Apple like fruit flies, choking the streets with their numbers, unaware or uncaring of one of the basic rules of Manhattan survival.

Pedestrians were not supposed to dawdle. And they were expected to ignore Walk and Don't Walk signs.

New Yorkers moved briskly from point A to point B and when they reached a street corner, they took one quick look and kept going. It was up to the trucks and taxis that hurtled down the streets to avoid them.

Tourists from Nebraska or Indiana and only-God-knew-where stopped and stared at the displays in department store windows in such numbers that they blocked the sidewalk. They formed a snaking queue around Radio City Music Hall, standing in the cold with the patience of dim-witted cattle. They clustered around the railing in Rockefeller Center, sighing over the too big, too gaudy, too everything Christmas tree that was the center's focal point.

As far as Dante was concerned, Scrooge had it right.

Bah, humbug, indeed, he thought as his chauffeur edged the big Mercedes through traffic.

The strange thing was, he'd never really noticed the inconvenience of the holiday until now. Basically, he'd never really noticed the holiday at all.

It was just another day.

As a child, Christmas had meant—if he were lucky—another third-hand winter jacket from the Jesuits that, you hoped, was warmer than the last. By the time he'd talked, connived and generally wheedled his way into a management job at a construction company where he'd spent a couple of years wielding a jackhammer, he was too busy to pay attention to the nonsense of canned carols and phony good cheer. And after he arrived in New York, earning the small fortune he'd needed to start building his own empire had taken all his concentration.

The last dozen years, of course, he'd had to notice Christmas. Not for himself but for others. Those with whom he did business and the ones who worked for him—the doormen, the elevator operators, the porters at the building in which he lived, all expected certain things of the holiday.

So Dante put in the requisite appearance at the annual

office party his P.A. organized. He authorized bonuses for his employees. He wrote checks for the doormen, the elevator operators and the porters. He thanked his P.A. for the bottle of Courvoisier she inevitably gave him and gave her, in return, a gift certificate to Saks.

Somehow, he'd never observed the larger picture.

Had tourists always descended on the city, inconveniencing everything and everyone? They must have.

Then, how could he not have noticed?

He was noticing now, all right. *Dio,* it was infuriating.

The Mercedes crept forward, then stopped. Crept forward, then stopped. Dante checked his watch, muttered a well-chosen bit of gutter Sicilian and decided he was better off walking.

"Carlo? I'm getting out. I'll call when I need you."

He opened the door to a dissonant blast of horns, as if a man leaving an already-stopped automobile might somehow impede the nonexistent flow of traffic. He slipped between a double-parked truck and a van, stepped onto the sidewalk and headed briskly toward the Fifth Avenue hotel where he was lunching with the owner of a private bank Russo International had just absorbed.

He'd be late. He hated that. Lateness was a sign of weakness.

Everything he did lately was a sign of weakness.

He was short-tempered. Impatient. Hell, there were times he was downright rude. And he was never that. Demanding, yes, but he asked as much of himself as he did of those who reported to him, but the past couple of weeks…

No. He'd be damned if he was going to think about that trip to Vermont again.

He thought about it too much already.

And the dreams that awakened him at night… What were they, if not an indication that he was losing his self-control?

Why would he dream about a woman he despised? For the same reason he'd kissed her, damn it. Because the ugly truth was that he still wanted her, despite her lies and her infidelity. Despite the fact that she'd borne another man's child. Nothing kept the dreams at bay. Each night, he imagined her coming to him, imagined stripping her naked, making love to her until she cried out in his arms and said, *Yes, Dante, yes, you make me feel things he never did.*

And awakened hard as stone, angry at himself for an adolescent's longings, for the frustration that he couldn't lose in another woman's bed though, God knew, he'd tried.

What an embarrassment that had been! *I'm sorry,* he'd said, *that's never happened to me before.*

It hadn't, though he doubted if the lady believed him. *He* could hardly believe it!

He was not himself since Vermont, and he didn't like it. One day in a snow-bound village and he'd discovered he was still an old-world *Siciliano* at heart, reacting to things with emotion instead of intellect.

How could a woman he didn't want ruin his sex life from a distance of four hundred miles?

Taylor had—what was the old saying? She'd put horns on his head, sleeping with another man while she was still his. She deserved whatever happened next.

She *had* been his, no matter what she claimed. So what if she hadn't let him pay her bills? If she hadn't lived with him?

She had belonged to him. He'd marked her with his hands. His mouth. His body.

And she'd let another man plant a seed in her womb. She'd given him a child. A child who should rightly have been—should rightly have been—

Dante frowned, gave himself a mental shake and prepared to vent his anger on the half a dozen idiots who'd come to a dead stop in the middle of the sidewalk.

"Excuse me," he said in a voice so frigid it made a mockery of the words.

Then he saw it wasn't only the people ahead of him. Nobody was moving. Well, yes. The crowd was shifting. Sideways, like a brontosaurus spying a fresh stand of leafy trees, heading for a huge, world-famous toy store.

Dante dug in his heels. "Excuse me," he said again. "Pardon me. Coming through."

Useless. Like a paper boat caught in a stream, the crowd herded him toward the doors.

"Wait a minute," he said to a massive woman with her elbow dug into his side. "Madam. I am not—"

But he was. Like it or not, Dante was swept inside.

A giant clock tower boomed out a welcome; a huge stuffed giraffe gave him the once-over. He was pushed past a tiger so big he half expected it to roar.

Somehow, weaving and bobbing, he worked to the edge of the crowd and found refuge behind a family of stuffed bears. He gave his watch one last glance, sighed and took out his cell phone.

"Traffic," he told the man he was to lunch with, in the tones of a put-upon New Yorker. It turned out the other man was still trapped in a taxi. They laughed and made plans for a drink that evening.

Dante put his phone away, folded his arms over his chest and settled in to wait for a break in the flow of parents and children so he could head for the door.

He didn't have to wait long. A trio of pleasantly efficient security guards cleared the way, formed the crowd into an orderly queue outside. Dante started toward the door, then fell back.

What a place this was!

And what would he have given to be turned loose in it when he was a boy. Just to look, to touch, would have been a time spent in paradise.

His toys had been stick swords. Newspaper kites. And, one magical Christmas Eve, an armless tin soldier he found in a dumpster while he scavenged for his supper.

How could he have forgotten that?

Oh, how he'd loved his soldier! He'd kept it safely buried in the pocket of his sagging jeans, bloodied the nose of a bigger boy who'd tried to steal it.

Was that what Taylor's daughter faced? Improvised toys? If she were lucky, a broken, discarded doll to call her own?

Dante scowled.

Talk about giving in to your emotions! The child—Samantha—was not the Poor Little Match Girl. Neither was her mother. Taylor was perfectly capable of earning a living.

Yes, he'd started the legal procedures that would take her house from her, but she'd reneged on the terms of the loan. It was business, plain and simple. She'd understood the risks when she signed those loan papers.

Besides, she wasn't destitute. She had possessions. She could sell them. She had friends in that town, people who'd help her and the child.

Then, why had her coat looked worn? The house, too. Even by candlelight, he could tell it needed work. The walls needed fresh paint. The wood floors needed refinishing. The furnishings were shabby. And where were the shiny, high-tech gadgets women always had in their kitchens?

Had Taylor deliberately simplified her life…or had fate done it for her?

A muscle flexed in his jaw.

Not that he cared. For every action, there was a reaction. That was basic science. She had deceived him, and he had repaid her.

The child was not his problem. Neither was Taylor. He had no regrets or remorse, and if her daughter didn't have a particularly merry Christmas this year…

Something bumped against his leg.

It was a child. A little girl, older than Samantha, clutching a cloth doll almost as big as she was in her arms.

"What did I tell you, Janey?" A harassed-looking woman caught the child's hand. "You can't see around that thing. Tell the man you're sorry."

"That's all right," Dante said quickly. "No harm done."

The child's mother smiled. "I told Janey that Santa's going to bring her some wonderful surprises in just a few weeks but she saw Raggedy Ann and, well, neither she or I could resist. You know?"

He didn't know, that was just the point. He'd never had surprises from Santa, never fallen in love with a goofy bear, like Samantha, or a rag doll like Janey.

Even if he had, who would have understood how important such a simple toy could be?

Dante watched the little girl and her mother fade into the crowd. He stood motionless, long after they'd disappeared from his sight.

Then he made his way out of the store, took out his cell phone to call his chauffeur... And, instead, called his P.A. to tell her he wasn't returning to the office.

He felt—what was the word? Unsettled. Perhaps he was coming down with something. Whatever the reason, walking to his apartment building on such a cold, crisp day might clear his head.

"You're home early, Mr. Russo," said his housekeeper when he stepped from the private elevator into the foyer of his penthouse.

Dante shrugged off his coat and told her he didn't want to be disturbed. Then he went into his study, turned on his computer and did what he could to further prepare for the meeting he'd have over drinks in just a few hours.

For the first time in his life, he couldn't get interested in the complex facts and figures of an imminent deal.

What kind of Christmas morning would Taylor and her child awaken to? There was a time he'd have assumed Taylor viewed the holiday with as much cynicism as he did. After all, he'd spent six months as her lover. He knew her. He knew her likes and dislikes...

Or did he?

She'd shown him a side of her he'd never suspected. Had she really grown up in a small town? If he hadn't seen her in that shabby little house with a child in her arms, even imagining Taylor in that kind of life would have been impossible.

People didn't even call her by that name in Shelby. She was Tally, not Taylor. A softer, more vulnerable name for a softer, more vulnerable woman.

Dante went to the window and looked down at Central Park. Thanks to the influx of out-of-towners, it was alive with people, even on a weekday afternoon. There were probably more people in the park right now than lived in the entire town of Shelby, Vermont.

If Taylor had stayed in New York, if she'd opened her business here, she'd be turning a handsome profit by now. She had contacts in the city, a reputation.

Dante watched the scene below him for long minutes. Children were sledding down a snowy incline; even from up here, he could see the bright flash of their snowsuits.

Would the little girl in the toy store find a sled under the tree Christmas morning?

Would Taylor's daughter?

A muscle knotted in his jaw.

No. The plan running through his head was clearly insane. She'd made a fool of him, wounded him in the worst way a woman can hurt a man.

But the child was innocent.

It was wrong, that children seemed always to pay for the sins of those who'd given them life.

The muscle in his jaw knotted again. Dante went to the breakfront, took out a bottle of brandy and poured an inch into a snifter. He warmed the glass between his palms, stared sightlessly into the rich depths of the swirling liquid.

And put it down, untouched.

Instead, he went to his desk. Picked up the phone. Made calls to his attorney, to his accountant, to the same private investigator who'd found Taylor for him.

If any of them thought his instructions were unusual, they knew better than to say so.

When he'd finished, Dante picked up his snifter of brandy and went up the spiral staircase to his suite.

The view was even better here. Three walls of glass gave him a vantage point a peregrine falcon would have as it swooped over the city.

Lights glimmered, diamonds sparkling against the pall of encroaching darkness, and he recalled the first time he'd stood here, gazing out into the night, the fierce swell of pride he'd felt at knowing all this was his, that his sweat, his struggles, his fight to get to the top had all been worth it.

Taylor had never seen this view. She'd come here for drinks, for dinner, but he'd never carried her up the stairs to this room.

To his bed.

Dante sipped the brandy.

What if he had? If he'd made love to her while the lights of the city challenged the stars in the night sky? If he'd taken her to these windows, naked. Stood with her as she looked out on his world. Stepped behind her. Cupped her breasts. Bent his head and kissed the skin behind her ear.

She'd always trembled when he kissed her there.

Trembled when he entered her.

He closed his eyes. Imagined entering her now, right now, here, as she looked into the night. Imagined holding her hips, pressing against her, the urgency of his erection seeking the heat, the silken dampness that was for him.

Only for him…

His eyes flew open.

The hell it was.

She'd been with another man, even while she'd been his because, damn it, she *had* belonged to him no matter what she said.

He turned from the window, turned from the images that assailed him.

What he'd just done had nothing to do with Taylor. It was simply an act of charity. This was the season for charity, after all. What he'd done was for a child. An innocent little girl, trapped in a game played by adults.

That the plan he'd set in motion would also bring Taylor back into his life was secondary. Whatever had happened between him and his once-upon-a-time lover was over.

Dante tossed back the rest of the brandy. The liquid burned its way down his throat and, as it did, burned him, as well, with the ugly truth.

Forget charity. Forget pretending that what had happened was over.

It wouldn't be. Not until he slept with the woman who'd made a fool of him, one last time.

CHAPTER SIX

WHEN SHE WAS SIX, Tally stopped believing in Santa Claus.

Her grandmother had taken her to the mall the week before. She'd been terrified of the man with the white beard and the booming laugh, but after a lot of coaxing, she'd sat in his lap and whispered that all she wanted for Christmas was a Pretty Patty doll.

Christmas Eve, she crept out of bed and saw her grandmother putting the doll under the tree.

Even then, she'd understood Grandma had to count every penny. That she'd loved Tally enough to buy the doll meant more than if Santa had brought it.

Now, twenty-two years later, she was close to believing in Santa again.

How else to explain the call from a decorator she'd worked with in Manhattan? He'd been in too much of a hurry to offer details but the bottom line was that he knew someone who knew someone who knew someone who was familiar with her work.

That person had recommended her for the commission of a lifetime.

"The guy's richer than Midas," Aston trilled. "Seems

he just bought out some old-line firm and the digs don't suit him, so he's moving the whole kit and caboodle to that new building on 57th and Mad. You know the one? Baby, this is one plum job! A huge budget, free creative rein... Pull this off, your name will blaze in neon!"

A couple of weeks back, Tally would have been flattered but she'd have turned down the offer. She'd have had no choice, not with a shop to open in Vermont. Now it seemed as if Dante's vicious act of revenge might turn out to be a godsend.

"He wants to meet with you first, of course. See if the synergy's right."

For an assignment like this, she'd do whatever it took to make the synergy right.

She splurged on a haircut, had her black suit cleaned and pressed, charged a new coat which she hated to do but appearance was everything in New York. If things went well, she'd be able to pay for it. If not, she was so broke that the credit card company would have to wait the next hundred years for their money.

She even tried to go back to thinking of herself as Taylor Sommers instead of Tally. Her given name had been the one she'd always used in the city. It suited the image she'd needed, that of a cool sophisticate.

The woman Dante had always assumed her to be. The one she knew he'd wanted her to be.

And yet, today, after leaving Samantha with Sheryl, riding the train into Manhattan, now standing across from the glass tower where she was to meet the Mystery Mogul, she felt more like Tally than Taylor.

Taylor wouldn't have butterflies swarming in her stomach.

Tally did.

She was nervous. Hell, she was terrified about meeting the man who held her future in his hands.

He had no name. Not yet.

"You know how these big shots are," Aston said. "Some of them won't make a move unless a camera's pointed at them, but some guard their privacy like lions protecting a kill. This guy's like that. He wants to stay nameless until the deal is struck."

The Mystery Mogul was meeting her in his new offices. Tally looked up, counting the floors even though she'd already done it twice, head tilted back like an out-of-towner.

The butterflies fluttered their wings again.

She wanted this job more than she'd ever wanted anything. Aston's description of it was almost too good to be true.

Her fee would be—well, enormous. More than she'd earn in five years in Shelby. She'd be able to give Sam everything. New toys, clothes, the best possible nanny to care for her while Tally was at work.

Best of all, she could deal with the loan payments she owed the bank—the payments she owed Dante. So much for his plans to destroy her.

She wouldn't even have to tackle the toughest thing about living in New York. The Mystery Mogul, it turned out, owned an apartment building with a two-bedroom, two-bath vacancy.

"Well, of course he does," Aston had said.

The way he said it made her laugh. It was the first time she'd laughed in weeks.

Since Dante's visit.

Since she'd discovered just how ruthless he could be.

Since she'd found out just how much she could hate him.

"The rent's a perk of the job, can you imagine?"

She could. A picture was emerging of a bona fide eccentric with money to burn. The only thing that almost stopped her was that this meant returning to Dante's city. And that was just plain ridiculous. It was her city, too, or had been for five years. Besides, the odds of running into one person in a city of eight million were zero to none.

And even if there was that eight-million-to-one chance, so what? She'd left Dante so he wouldn't know she was having his baby, but it turned out she needn't have worried. She'd told him Sam wasn't his and he'd been only too willing to believe her.

Tally lifted her chin as she strode through the lobby of the glass tower and stepped into a waiting elevator. She should have spat in his face that night in her kitchen. Given the opportunity a second time, she wouldn't pass it by.

"To hell with you, Dante Russo," she said aloud, as the elevator whisked her to the twenty-seventh floor. "You're a cold, contemptible son of a bitch and—"

The doors slid open.

And the cold, contemptible son of a bitch was standing in front of her, arms folded, face expressionless.

"Hello, Taylor," he said, and that was when she knew she'd been had. All this—the wonderful job, the money, the apartment...

It was all a cruel joke.

A joke only one of them could laugh at, she thought,

and then she stopped thinking, called him a word she had never before thought, much less used, and launched herself at the man she would hate for the rest of her life.

DANTE HAD KNOWN this wouldn't be easy.

Taylor despised him. Well, so what? The feeling was mutual.

And she was proud.

He admired that in her; he always had. She'd never shown the weakness so many women—hell, so many men and women—showed, that of needing someone to lean on. Like him, she was independent and strong.

But things had changed.

She did need someone now. Some no-good SOB had gotten her pregnant and walked away, left her with a child to raise, and that made all the difference.

He'd decided to start by telling her that but she didn't give him the chance. The elevator doors opened, she saw who was waiting for her and she came at him like a tiger.

He got his arms up just in time to keep her from clawing his face.

"Taylor," he said, "Taylor, listen—"

"No," she panted, raining blows on his upraised arms, "I'm done listening, you bastard! Wasn't what you did to me enough? Did you need an encore? You no-good, heartless—"

He caught her hands, yanked them behind her back. "Stop it!"

"Let go. You let go of me or—"

She was still fighting him. Dante grunted, tucked his shoulder down and hoisted her over it like a bag of laundry. She shrieked, kicked her feet and yanked at his hair. What in hell would he say if somebody came running to see who was being murdered?

"Put me down!"

"With pleasure," he said grimly.

The former tenants had left behind a couple of chairs, half a dozen file cabinets and a small black leather sofa. Dante strode to it and dumped her on it. Then he stood back, folded his arms again and glared.

What had made him think helping her would be a good idea?

"Don't even think about it," he warned when she scrambled up against the cushions.

"I hate you, Dante. Do you hear me? I hate you!"

"I'd never have known."

She sat up straight, mouth trembling. "How even *you* could do something like this, you—you—"

"Watch what you say, *cara*."

"Do not call me that!"

"Is it your habit to attack your clients?"

"If you think I'm going to be party to this—this schoolboy prank—"

"You're so sure you know everything, Taylor. Is it possible you don't?"

"I know what you are. That's all that's necessary."

She rose to her feet, tugged down her coat, smoothed her hands over her hair. She was still shaking and suddenly he wanted to go to her, take her in his arms and tell her everything was going to be all right. That he would take care of her.

Except, that wasn't why he'd brought her here. It was for the child.

And for yourself, a voice in his head said slyly. How

come he'd forgotten his vow to sleep with this woman one last time? That would put her out of his thoughts forever. He didn't need to hear her say she wanted him. Or that she was sorry she'd been unfaithful. He didn't need to hear the words she'd whispered that night three years ago when she'd begged him to stay with her, to stay in her arms, in her bed.

"Get out of my way!"

She was looking up at him as if she wanted to kill him. Fine. The game he'd planned was one that was best played by sworn enemies.

"We'll have our meeting first."

"We've already had it. To think you'd resort to such— to such subterfuge, just so you could make a fool of me!"

"Would you have agreed to this appointment if you'd known I was the man involved?"

"You know I wouldn't." Her eyes filled with angry tears. "Why did you do it? You're taking my house. My livelihood. What more do you want?"

He wasn't going to answer. She could tell by the way he was looking at her but it didn't matter. She already knew the answer. What he'd done to her wasn't sufficient. He wanted to give the knife one more twist.

How? she thought bitterly. How could she have made love with a man like this? How could she have even believed she'd fallen in love with him? Because she had believed it, yes. That was why she'd left him, because she knew he didn't love her, wouldn't love the child they'd created together. She'd left rather than see him look at her as he was looking at her now, as if she had no meaning to him at all.

She took a deep breath, drew what remained of her pride around her like a ragged cloak and started past him.

"Taylor."

She shook her head. She had nothing left to say to him.

His hand closed on her wrist. "You asked me questions. Are you going to leave before you hear the answers?"

She looked pointedly from his hand to hers. "Let go."

"I didn't bring you to New York on false pretenses."

She laughed. "You didn't, huh?"

"Isn't that what I just said?"

"Well, let's see. You got someone to offer me a commission decorating these offices. He mentioned a budget big enough to make my head spin. Oh, and he said there'd be an apartment with the rent a perk of the job." Tally tugged her hand free and put her hands on her hips. "If those aren't false pretenses—"

"The offer is real. All of it. The commission, the budget, the place to live."

Everything from shock to distrust to outright utter disbelief showed in her face. He tucked his hands in his trouser pockets and kept his tone as flat as his eyes.

"It's all yours, if you want it."

She stared at him. "Why?"

"There's an old saying about not looking a gift horse in the mouth."

"I know the saying. Maybe it lost something in the translation. What it means is that an unexpected gift is a gift to beware of."

Dante took a deep breath. "The child," he said.

"What child?" Tally felt her heart beat quicken. Did he know? Had he somehow learned the truth of her pregnancy? "You mean—you mean Sam?"

He nodded. "Yes."

"What about her?"

"I've had time to think." A muscle flexed in his jaw. "And I realized that it's wrong to punish her for your behavior."

He didn't know. Tally almost sagged with relief.

"Your daughter is innocent of all that happened. You deceived me. You left me. But none of that is her doing. The world is filled with children who suffer because of the behavior of adults. I see no reason to add to their number."

She stared at him. Dante Russo, showing compassion to a little girl he thought had been fathered by another man? Why would he show compassion at all? All the months they'd been lovers, she'd waited, she'd yearned to see some show of human emotion in this man.

She never had.

Oh, he supported charities. Smiled at things that were amusing. Frowned at things that were annoying.

But he never lost his composure. Not even in bed.

Not that he wasn't an incredible lover. He was. Alert to her every sigh, her every unspoken desire. He'd given her more pleasure than she'd ever imagined possible.

The way he moved inside her.

The way he brought her to climax.

And yet, he'd always been in control. Always, except that one night when he'd been as tender as he was wild, when she'd asked him to stay with her.

When she'd conceived Samantha.

"Well?"

Tally blinked. Dante was looking at her with barely veiled impatience.

"You asked me why I'd offer this assignment to you and I told you the reason. It's your turn now. Will you accept it? Or will you turn it down because I'm the man making the offer?"

Something was wrong. She felt as if she were looking at a jigsaw puzzle with one piece—the key piece—missing.

"Yes or no?"

She almost laughed. The imperious tone of voice. The straight posture. The cold eyes that said, "I'm in command."

Except, he wasn't.

He couldn't order her around. She wouldn't permit it. She had to think. Nothing was happening the way it was supposed to. She'd worried about being in the same city with this man and now it turned out she'd be working for him.

Impossible.

Better to go home…and do what? Lose the house? Move to a furnished room? Take whatever job she could find? Earn barely enough to live on and, oh yes, impose on Sheryl's kindness by asking her to watch Sam?

"Taylor, I want an answer!"

There was only one answer, but she couldn't bring herself to give it. Not without making him wait.

"I'll call you with my decision."

His eyes narrowed. She tried to move past him as quickly as possible, but his hand clamped down on her shoulder.

"Would you put your pride before the welfare of your daughter?"

"Nice, Dante. Really nice." Tally's eyes blazed with anger. "Don't you try and lay this on me! I never ignored Sam's welfare and I sure as hell never tripped over my own oversize ego! You're the one who came to Shelby, who bought a bank just so you could tear my child's life to pieces."

"That wasn't my intention."

"Maybe not, but it's what you did."

"Yes. And now, I intend to undo it. I will not avenge myself by hurting a child."

"My God, listen to you! So high and mighty. So godlike. Anyone would think you have a conscience. Maybe even a heart."

"Damn you, Taylor!" His fingers dug into her flesh as he pulled her to him. "I want to do the right thing. Why make it so difficult?"

And, in that moment, it came to her. The missing piece of the puzzle. What he'd just called doing the right thing. If that was his intention, there was a much easier way to do it. Why wasn't he taking it?

"If you're serious about not wanting my little girl to pay the price of your revenge—"

"Interesting," he said silkily, "how you manage to misquote me, *cara*. I said I would not avenge myself through her. We both know what that means, that your daughter should not pay the price of your unfaithfulness."

"Put whatever twist you like on it. The point is, if you've suddenly turned into the male counterpart of Mother Teresa, why go through all this? Why not simply stop the foreclosure proceedings?"

There it was, the million-dollar question. The question he'd asked himself a dozen times since coming up with this idea. His attorney and his accountant, each of whom knew only small details of the overall situation, had finally asked it, too, but he hadn't given them any explanations.

A man who answered to no one but himself didn't have to.

That didn't mean it wasn't a damned good question. All he had to do was have the loan payments rescheduled. Or tear up the documents altogether.

End of problem.

Nothing else made sense. Not to his attorney, to his accountant, to him and now to Taylor, who was looking at him with her eyebrows arched.

Dante frowned. She could look at him any way she liked. He didn't owe her an explanation, either.

"It's too complicated to explain."

Her smile was thin. "Try."

"There are banking laws. Rules. And I've already set the foreclosure procedure in motion."

"And I'll unset it by repaying the loan with my earnings from this job." Another thin smile. "Try again."

For a second, he looked blank. "You'd see it as charity. You'd never accept it."

It was a good save. The sudden lift of her eyebrows told him so.

"This way, you'll work for the money," he said, feeling his way carefully through the explanation that had suddenly come to him and knowing it was flawed. Give her too much time, she'd realize that. "I'm simply offering you a practical way out of your dilemma."

Yes, Tally thought. That was how it seemed—but then, the fly that had wandered into the spider's parlor had probably thought she was being asked in for a cup of tea.

And yet, what was the alternative? Could she really say no to his offer and condemn Samantha to financial uncertainty? Besides that, he was right. She'd be working for this money. No favors given, no favors asked.

"Well?"

She looked up. Dante was scowling. Obviously, he had none of her reservations about them being in close contact.

"I can't spend the entire day at this, Taylor. I need an answer. Will you take the job or won't you?"

She took a deep, steadying breath. "I'll take it."

Something flashed in his eyes. Triumph, she thought, but then it was gone, he was smiling politely and holding out his hand. She stared at it. Then, carefully, she extended her hand, too, felt his callused palm against hers as they shook hands.

"I want certain assurances," she said quickly.

"We've already sealed the deal. But go ahead. I'll try and accommodate you. What assurances do you want?"

"Our relationship will be strictly business."

He didn't say anything. His expression didn't change. Was that agreement or was he waiting to hear more?

"Our meetings will occur in public places."

"Such logical choices, *cara*. I'm impressed. Is that all?"

"No. It isn't." She folded her arms. "You're not to call me that."

"What? *Cara?*" He laughed. "You're my employee. I'll call you anything I like."

"I'm not your employee. We'll be working together. Either way, calling me *cara* would be improper."

He smiled, and her heart rose into her throat because everything she'd feared about him, everything she'd adored about him, was in that smile.

"Ah. I understand now." He cupped her elbows.

Slowly, inexorably, he drew her closer. "You're afraid our relationship will become personal."

"It won't," she said stiffly. "How could it, when you're the last man on earth I'd want to become personal with?"

"I used to call you *cara* when you were in my arms. When I was making love to you."

Taylor's breath caught. The sound of his voice at those moments. The feel of his hands on her breasts. The darkness of his eyes as he'd slipped his hands beneath her, as he entered her. Slowly, so slowly, until she cried out with pleasure at the feel of him deep, deep inside her...

"No," she said, "I don't remember. Why would I? It meant nothing. It meant—It meant—"

Dante stopped her lies with a kiss.

Fight him, she thought desperately, *don't let him do this to you.*

But the terrible truth was, he was doing what she had dreamed of. What she ached for. She loved the feel of his mouth on hers. The scent of his skin. The way he moved his hands down her spine and lifted her against him so that his erection pressed against her belly.

"Kiss me back," he said, his voice a rough command, and her treacherous body responded, her lips parted and when they did, he thrust his tongue into her mouth and she felt it happening as it always did, her breasts swelling, her bones melting, her body readying for his possession...

Her heart yearning for what he would never give her.

Tally wrenched free of his embrace.

"No." Her voice was hoarse. "I don't want that from you. Not anymore."

He said nothing for a long moment. Then he let go of her.

"As you wish."

"As I insist."

"Please," he said coolly, "no ultimatums. You made your point. And now…"

He glanced at his watch, then plucked his cell phone from his pocket and made a brief call. It was like a slap in the face, a way of telling her that the kiss had meant nothing to him.

"I've arranged for my driver to come for you."

"That's not necessary. My hotel—"

"I've checked you out of your hotel." His hand clasped her elbow; he moved her into the elevator with determined efficiency. "Carlo will take you to your rooms."

"Rooms?" she said, as the elevator plunged toward the lobby. "Aston said an apartment."

"The rooms for you and your daughter are a separate suite within an apartment."

"Whose apartment?" Tally said, heart suddenly racing.

His eyes met hers. "Mine," he answered.

Before she could respond, the doors swept open on the lobby and Dante handed her over to his waiting driver.

CHAPTER SEVEN

DID HE REALLY THINK she'd live in his apartment?

Not even if the alternative was a tent pitched in the Millers' backyard.

Tally let Dante's driver take her to Central Park West but only because she had to go there if she wanted to reclaim her luggage.

She'd get it, write the imperious Mr. Russo a note telling him, in exquisite detail, what he could do with his contract, phone for a taxi and leave. No. This time, she'd face him. She would not forgo that pleasure.

The driver was new but the doorman was the same as in the past. He greeted her by name, as if three long years had not gone by since her last visit. So did the house-keeper, who added that it was good to see her again.

"This way, miss," she said pleasantly, gesturing not to the library or the dining room or the sitting room, all the places—the only places—Tally had seen when she and Dante had been involved, but to the graceful, winding staircase.

"Thank you," Tally said, "but I'll wait for Mr. Russo in the library. If someone would just bring me my suitcase...?"

"Your things are already upstairs, miss. I'll show you to your rooms."

Arguing seemed pointless. Her quarrel was with Dante, not with his staff. She followed the housekeeper to a door that led into a sitting room as large as her entire house back in Vermont.

"Would you like some tea, miss?"

What she'd have liked was some strychnine for her host, but Tally managed a polite smile.

"Nothing, thank you."

"Ellen's unpacked your things. If you're not pleased with how she's arranged your clothes, just ring."

But I'm not staying, Tally started to say, except, by then the housekeeper had disappeared.

Dante wasn't just arrogant, he was presumptuous. She could hardly wait to see him and tell him so, but where was he? And when was the last train to Shelby? Eight? Nine? She intended to be on it. No way could she afford a night in a hotel now that her prospective job had turned out to be a farce.

Tally took out her cell phone and dialed Sheryl to see how Sam was and to tell her that the plans that had seemed so magical had fallen apart, but there was no answer. What a time to be reminded that cell service in Shelby wasn't always what you hoped.

Was nothing going to go right today?

Twenty minutes passed. Thirty. Tally frowned. Paced the sitting room. Checked her watch again. Damn it, she didn't have time for this! She'd wait another half hour, then give up the pleasure of confronting Mr. Russo and his monumental ego.

Getting on that train, getting back to Sam and the real

world, was more important. In fact, why was she wasting time waiting for Dante when she could be packing? She didn't need a maid to toss things into a suitcase.

Chin lifted, Tally marched through the sitting room, though a light-filled bedroom, to a door she assumed led to a closet…

Her breath caught.

The door didn't open on a closet. It opened on a room meant for a very lucky little girl.

For Samantha.

The walls were painted cream and decorated with murals that spoke of fairy tales, princesses and unicorns. The carpet was pale pink. The crib and furniture were cream and gold. A rocker stood near the window, a patchwork afghan draped over it. Tucked away in one corner, a playhouse shaped like a castle rose toward the ceiling, guarded by a family of plush teddy bears.

The room was a little girl's dream.

For a heartbeat, Tally's mood softened. She could imagine her daughter's excitement at such wonders.

Then she came to her senses and saw the room for what it really was.

Did Dante think he could bribe her into staying?

She turned on her heel. There was nothing she'd brought to the city she couldn't do without. To hell with packing. To hell with confronting Dante. All she wanted was to go home.

Quickly she left the suite, went down the stairs and headed straight for the private elevator…

But it was already there.

The doors slid open just as she reached them and she saw Dante standing in the mahogany and silver car.

Dante, with Samantha curled in his arms.

The blood drained from Tally's head.

Of all the things she'd imagined happening this day, she'd never envisioned this. Not this. Not her former lover, with his daughter in his arms.

Sam was so fair. Dante was so dark. And yet—oh, God—and yet they were so right together. The same softly curling hair. The same wide eyes and firm mouths, curving in the same smiles as they looked at each other, Dante with a softness of expression Tally had never seen in his face before, Sam babbling happily about something in a two-year-old's combination of real and made-up words.

Dante and Samantha. A father and his daughter.

The ground tilted under Tally's feet.

Blindly she stuck out a hand in a search for support. She must have made a sound because suddenly Dante looked up and saw her.

His smile faded. *"Cara?"*

I'm fine, she said. Or tried to say. But the words wouldn't come, nothing would come but another soft sound of distress. Dante barked a command. His housekeeper ran into the room, took Sam from him, and then it was Tally who was in Dante's arms, his strong arms, and he was carrying her swiftly through the apartment.

"Cara," he said again, "Tally…"

He had never called her that before. She thought of how soft the name sounded on his lips. Of how the world was spinning, spinning, spinning…

And then everything went black.

WHEN SHE OPENED HER EYES, she was in an enormous, canopied bed in a softly lit room.

Where was she? What had happened? Something

terrible. Something that carried within it the seeds of disaster.

She sat up against a bank of silk-covered pillows—and everything came rushing back. Dante. Samantha. Her baby in her lover's arms. Her baby, here, in this place, where three years' worth of secrets might untangle like a skein of yarn.

Tally started to push the comforter aside. She had to find Sam. Take her home...

"*Cara.* What are you doing?"

Dante's voice was harsh. He stood in the door between the bath and the bedroom, his tall, powerful figure shadowy in the light.

"Where's my baby?"

"Samantha is fine."

He came toward her, a glass of water in one hand, a small tablet in the other. Tally brushed aside his out-stretched hand.

"Where is she?"

"She's in the nursery. Asleep."

"I want to see her."

"I told you, she's fine."

Tally swung her feet to the floor. "Don't argue with me, Dante! I want to see her now."

"The tablet first."

She glared up at him. She knew him well; enough to know he wasn't going to let her get past him until she obeyed his command.

"What is that?"

"Just something to calm you."

"I don't need calming, damn it!"

"The doctor disagreed."

"You called a doctor?"

"Of course I did," he said brusquely. "You fainted."

"Only because—because I was stunned to see my daughter. You had no right—"

"Take the tablet." His mouth twitched. "Then you can tell me what a monster I am, for flying Samantha here so she could be with you."

She glared at him one last time. Then she snatched the glass from his hand, dumped the tablet in her mouth and gulped it down with a mouthful of water.

Tell him what a monster he was? No. She wasn't going to waste the time. You couldn't argue with Dante Russo. He was always right, so why bother? She'd take Sam and leave.

But first, she had to get dressed.

The realization that she was *undressed* surged through her. She was wearing a nightgown of pale blue silk, its thin straps scattered with pink silk rosebuds, the kind of gown only a man would buy for a woman.

An ache, sharp as a knife, pierced her heart. Was the woman Dante had bought it for as lovely as the gown? She must have been, for him to have given her something so fragile and exquisitely beautiful. For him to have made love to that woman here, in his home, where he had never made love to her.

Unaccountably, her eyes stung with tears. Angry tears. What else could they be?

Damn Dante Russo to hell! Who had given him permission to have his housekeeper take off her clothes and dress her in this gown that wasn't hers?

"Well?"

She looked up. Dante was watching her, one dark eyebrow raised.

"Aren't you going to tell me I'm a monster?"

"Get away from me," Tally said, her voice trembling.

"After all," he said, a wry smile curving his lips, "you have every reason to despise me. You pass out, I phone for my doctor.... What woman wouldn't hate a man under those circumstances?"

"I want my clothes."

"Why?"

"Dante. You may find this amusing, but I do not. You seem to think you can—you can take control of my life. Well, you can't. I don't want your job. I don't want your guest suite. I don't want you thinking you can decide what's best for my baby, I don't want your housekeeper undressing me, and I certainly do not want your mistress's cast-offs."

"Such a long list of don'ts," he said mildly, tucking his hands into the pockets of what she now realized were soft-looking gray sweatpants. "Unfortunately, not all of them are appropriate."

"Damn you, I'm not playing games!"

"Let's go through them one by one, shall we?"

"Let's not. I told you—"

"I heard you. Now it's your turn to listen. Number one, I'm not trying to control anything. You agreed to the terms of the job."

"If by 'terms,' you mean me living in your home—"

"Two," he said, ignoring her protests, "I cannot imagine that thinking it best for you and Sam to be together as soon as possible was a mistake."

"I was going home to her. Didn't that occur to you?"

"It did, but I have a private plane. Why would you want to spend hours on the train, only to turn around and make the trip here again when I could arrange to bring her to you tonight?"

"Damn it, who gave you the right to think for me? I was not going to turn around, as you put it, and make the trip here again. I told you, I don't want your—"

"And, finally," he said, "finally, *cara,* you're wrong about the nightgown." He took his hands from his pockets, reached out and trailed one finger deliberately across one rose-embroidered strap, hooking the tip under the fabric, lightly tugging at it so that she had no choice but to sit forward. "I bought it for you, along with some other things I thought you might need to help you settle in." His voice turned silken. "And then there's that final accusation. That my housekeeper undressed you. She didn't."

A rush of color shot into Tally's face. Dante saw it and smiled.

"Why would I have her do that," he said softly, "when I've undressed you myself hundreds of times in the past?"

"The past is dead, Dante. You had no right—"

"Damn it," he said sharply, his smile vanishing, "who are you to talk about rights?" His hands cupped her shoulders and he drew her to her feet. "Such self-righteous garbage from a woman who ran like a coward instead of facing a man and telling him she'd cheated on him!"

"I didn't—"

"What? You didn't cheat? What do you call becoming involved with another man, if not cheating? Come on, Tally. I'd love to hear you come up with a better word."

What could she say to that? Nothing, not without admitting the truth. Telling him he'd fathered Sam would open her to his scorn, his anger and, worst of all, to the possibility he'd try and take her daughter from her.

"That's a fine speech," she said calmly, even though her heart was racing. "But you're only making it because I wounded your ego. You were bored. You were going to leave me. Instead, I made the first move. That's what really bothers you and you know it."

Was it? She'd just told him exactly what he'd been telling himself for three years, but now he wasn't sure it was that simple. Had he planned on breaking things off because he was bored, or was there some deeper reason he hadn't wanted to face?

Was that what had driven her into the arms of a stranger?

Maybe he'd ask himself that question someday, but not now. Not when all his rage at Tally had turned to fear an hour ago, when he'd watched her face whiten as she crumpled to the floor.

Now she stood straight and tall before him, her eyes fixed on his and glittering with unshed, angry tears. Her hair was loose; he'd undone the pins himself, let it tumble to her shoulders in soft, heavy waves. She wore no makeup; he'd washed it away with a cool cloth and it occurred to him that he'd never seen her like this before, that in all the time they'd been lovers, her appearance had always been perfect.

She'd been beautiful then but she was even more lovely like this, he'd thought, her lips naked of artificial color, her hair in sweet disarray. She was what they called her in Vermont.

She was Tally, not Taylor, and something in the softness of the old-fashioned name had made his throat constrict.

Slowly, he'd undressed her, telling himself it was only so he didn't have to ring for Mrs. Tipton or Ellen.

His hands had trembled as he undid the buttons of her suit, as he slid her blouse from her shoulders.

It was so long since he'd seen her breasts. Her belly. The pale curls that hid the sweet folds of flesh where he longed to bury himself. The long legs that had once wrapped around his hips as he lost himself in her welcoming heat.

And yet, despite those images, what he'd felt, undressing Tally, hadn't been sexual desire.

What he'd felt was the desire to protect her. To hold her close. Rock her in his arms. Tell her he was sorry he'd hurt her, sorry he hadn't understood what she'd needed of him, what he'd needed of her all those years ago....

"Even now," Tally said, her voice tinged with bitterness, "even now, you can't tell me the truth."

"You're right," he said quietly. "I was going to leave you." Tally turned away. He cupped her jaw and forced her to meet his eyes. "But I don't know why, *cara*. I thought that I did, but now I'm not so sure." His gaze fell to her lips. "All I'm sure of is this."

"No," she whispered, but even as he lowered his head to hers, Tally didn't pull back. She shut her eyes, felt the whisper of his breath on her mouth, and when he gathered her into his arms and said her name, she moaned and melted against him.

This was the kind of kiss they'd shared on the night that had changed everything. It was a kiss of tenderness and longing so intense she could feel his heart thudding against hers and with a suddenness that stunned her, she knew she wanted more.

"Dante," she said, the word a soft sigh against his lips. "Dante…"

His name, breathed against his mouth. Her breasts, pressed to his chest. Her belly, soft against his. Dante groaned, slid his hands into Tally's spill of cinnamon hair and gathered her closer.

Passion exploded between them.

Tenderness became desire; longing turned to desperate need. Dante's mouth demanded acquiescence and Tally give it, parting her lips so his tongue could seek out her honeyed taste. He groaned, slid down the delicate straps of the nightgown, baring her breasts to his hands and mouth.

"Say it," he demanded, and she did.

Her whispered "Yes, make love to me. Yes, touch me, yes, yes, yes," rose into the silence of the winter night and filled him with ecstasy.

And he knew, in that instant, that taking her to bed once more in a quest for revenge was not what he needed at all.

He needed her wanting him, like this. Crying out as he bent to her and sucked her nipple deep into his mouth. Tossing her head back in frenzied response to the brush of his hand as he dragged up the skirt of her gown, cupped her mons with his palm, felt her hot tears of desire damp on his fingers and sweet heaven, he was going to come, to come, to come…

He scooped Tally into his arms.

"Now," he said fiercely, his mouth at her throat, and she sobbed his name over and over as he carried her through the vast room, heading not to her bed but to his…

A child's voice cried out.

"Sam," Tally whispered.

Dante shut his eyes. Dragged air into his lungs. Turned and carried her to the nursery, where he set her gently on her feet.

He stood back and let her approach the child in the white and gold crib alone.

"Baby," she murmured, "did you have a bad dream?"

"Mama?"

Tally lifted her daughter in her arms. Sam was warm from sleep, sweet from the mingled scents of soap and baby powder. She sighed and laid her head against Tally's shoulder.

"Teddies are sleepin', Mama."

Teddies, indeed. The bedraggled, much-loved bear from home sat in the corner of the crib, side by side with the smallest new teddy from the bear family Dante had bought.

Unaccountably, Tally's heart swelled.

"Yes, baby," she said softly, "I see."

She went to the rocking chair, sat in it and gently rocked Sam back and forth, back and forth.

"'Hush little baby,'" she sang softly, "'don't you cry…'"

Gradually, Samantha's breathing slowed. Tally waited until she was certain she was sound asleep. Then she carried her child to the crib, laid her in it, covered her with a blanket and pressed a kiss to her hair.

When she turned she saw Dante, still in the doorway, watching her, his face unreadable in the soft shadows cast by the nightlight.

Oh, Dante, she thought, *Dante…*

Slowly, she went to him and looked into his eyes. A muscle jumped in his cheek. He lifted his hand and reached toward her and she shook her head and pulled back, knowing that if he touched her—if he touched her...

"What we did—what we almost did—was a mistake."

"Making love is never a mistake, *cara*."

He was wrong. It was a mistake, and Tally knew it. Knew it because she'd finally faced the truth.

She loved Dante Russo with all her heart.

Bad enough she could never tell him she'd borne him a child, but to lie in his arms and pretend it was only sex would be the ultimate travesty.

A heart could only be broken so many times before it shattered into a million pieces.

Tally put her hands lightly on Dante's chest. "Maybe not," she said softly. "But it can't happen anymore."

A smile tilted at the corners of his mouth. "Does this mean I won't have to sue you for breach of contract?"

She smiled, too. "If you mean, will I take the job, the answer is yes. It's a wonderful opportunity, and I thank you for it. And I'll stay here." Her voice grew soft. "This suite is beautiful, and the nursery you created for Sam is a little girl's dream come true." She drew a breath. "But you have to give me your word you won't try to make love to me."

"Is that really what you want?"

No. Oh no, it wasn't. She longed to tell him that, to go into his arms, lift her mouth to his, plead for him to carry her to bed and love her until dawn lit the sky....

"*Cara?* Is it really what you want?"

She had lied to him already. Now she had no choice but to lie to him again.

"Yes."

Long seconds dragged by. Then Dante took her hand, pressed a kiss to the palm and folded her fingers over it.

It was only hours later, as she lay in bed watching dawn slip over the city, that Tally realized Dante hadn't actually said he'd agree.

CHAPTER EIGHT

TALLY WAS UP at six the next morning.

Sam was still asleep in the next room, sprawled on her belly in her new crib, flanked by both her teddy bears.

Tally smiled, bent down and pressed a light kiss to her daughter's hair. Then she showered, put on a clean blouse but the same black suit and took a critical look at herself in the mirror.

She needed to buy clothes. If you looked successful, people assumed that you were. It wasn't the best way to judge anyone but that was how it went, especially in this town.

Her pay would be based partly on salary and expenses, partly on the cost of the completed project. So far, no one had mentioned when she'd get a check. She hated to ask, especially because it was Dante she'd have to go to, but she'd have to work up to it, and soon.

Tally gave her image another glance, then took a deep breath. Maybe she'd be lucky and Dante would already have left for the day.

No such luck.

He was in the sun-filled breakfast room, seated at

a round glass table with a cup of black coffee in his hand and the business section of the *New York Times* in front of him.

He looked up as Tally entered, and half rose from his chair. She motioned him to stay seated and went to the sideboard to pour herself coffee. It was easier to do that than to think about the fact that this was the very first time they'd had breakfast together.

"Good morning," he said. "Did you sleep well?"

She nodded. "Fine, thank you." A lie, of course. She'd tossed half the night, thinking of him in a room just down the stairs. "Thank you, too, for having that baby intercom installed between my room and Sam's."

"No problem. Actually, I had monitors installed throughout the place. I thought it would make you feel more comfortable, knowing you could hear Samantha no matter where you were."

"That was very thoughtful," she said politely, and sipped at her coffee.

"Sit down and join me."

There was no way to turn down the request, especially since he'd risen to his feet and was pulling out the chair opposite his. She thanked him, slipped into the chair and tried to concentrate on the coffee. It wasn't an easy thing to do.

Dante was a major distraction.

He was—there was no other word for it—he was beautiful. Not in a feminine way but beautiful all the same, wearing what she knew was a custom-made dark-blue suit, a pale-blue shirt from the city's most distinguished shirtmaker, and a maroon silk tie. His dark hair was curling and damp from the shower.

Another first.

They'd never breakfasted together, and she'd never seen him fresh from the shower. They'd had long bouts of incredible sex but afterward, he'd always dressed and gone home to shower. He preferred his own things, he'd told her. His soap, his razor, his toiletries, and she'd understood that what he'd really meant was that sex was one thing but showering was another, that he would only take intimacy just so far....

"Tally?"

She blinked. Dante had pushed a vellum envelope and a leather-bound notebook toward her.

"Sorry." She gave a polite little laugh. "I was—I was just trying to plan my day."

"I've already planned some of it for you. I hope you don't mind, but I want you to get up to speed as quickly as possible."

"Oh. Oh, no. I want that, too."

"There's a check in the envelope. Call it a signing bonus. If it isn't enough—"

"I'm sure it'll be fine. Thank you."

"Don't thank me. You're going to work hard to earn your money. You'll find your appointments for today listed in the notebook. For right now—" Dante glanced at his watch, pushed back his chair and rose to his feet "—I have to get going. Carlo will take you to the office."

"Your driver? Won't you need him?"

"I'm flying to Philadelphia. I'll take a cab to the airport."

Philadelphia. How long would he be gone? Would he be back by evening? It was better if he weren't. Then she wouldn't have to imagine returning here, seeing him, saying something banal as she went to the guest suite and he went out because he would go out, wouldn't he? There had to be a woman in his life. He was too virile a man to be without one.

But if there were, would he have kissed *her?* Would he have said he wanted to make love to her? Would he look at her as he had last night, as if he could almost feel her in his arms, hear her moans, because she would moan if he touched her, and—what was wrong with her today? She couldn't live here and imagine these things.

"Tally?"

"Yes?"

"You seem…distracted."

Heat rushed to her face. "No, not at all." Quickly, to cover her embarrassment, she added, "You said you're flying to Philadelphia?"

"And that my P.A., Joan, will show you around. She took care of furnishing your office. If it doesn't please you, tell her to make whatever changes you wish. Joan's also the one who scheduled your appointments, so if you have any questions—"

"Ask Joan."

Dante nodded and walked around the table to where she sat.

"She's organized meetings for you with half a dozen prospective assistants."

He was leaning over her; his scent drifted to her. Soap, water and pure, sexy essence of Dante. That was how she'd always thought of the smell of his skin. She'd never forgotten it or the memories it evoked.

His taste on her tongue. The feel of him, under her hands.

"I'm right," he said softly.

Tally looked up. His face was close to hers, his eyes a deep, cool gray.

"Something's definitely distracting you, *cara*. What could it be?"

"Nothing. I'm just—I'm concentrating on what you said. My office. Appointments with possible assistants. What else?"

"Did Mrs. Tipton tell you that she and Ellen will be happy to look after Sam, until you've hired a nanny?"

He leaned closer. All she had to do was turn her head an inch and her lips would brush his jaw.

"She told me. That's very—" she cleared her throat "—that's very kind of them. I'll contact an agency first thing and—"

"Joan's already taken care of it. A highly recommended agency is sending over half a dozen women for you to interview. They all have impeccable credentials, but again, if you're not satisfied, all you need do is inform Joan."

His shoulder brushed hers. Was it her imagination, or could she feel the heat of him through all the layers of clothing separating them?

"Tally? Is that acceptable?"

His eyes were on hers. The color had gone from gray to silver. Silver that somehow burned like flame.

"It's—it's fine."

"Because," he said, his voice suddenly low and husky, "because, *cara,* we can always alter the arrangement we made."

He wasn't talking about the office or her appointments, and they both knew it.

"No," she said, "we can't. I want things exactly as we agreed."

"Are you certain?"

The only thing she was certain of was that she had to get herself under control because she couldn't do this. Think about him making love to her, want him making love to her...

She took a deep breath. "Yes."

"In that case, there's nothing left to do this morning." His gaze dropped to her lips. "Except this," he said softly, and brushed his mouth over hers.

"No," she said, hating the soft, breathless quality of her voice.

"You're starting a new career and I'm flying to an important meeting. It's just a kiss for luck. Surely, I'm allowed that?"

"Dante. We can't—"

"We aren't."

He put his hand under her chin, lifted her face and claimed her mouth with his. And she—she let it happen. Let him slide the tip of his tongue between her lips, let him thrust his fingers into her hair, let him deepen the kiss until she was dizzy with wanting him....

Dante let go of her, straightened and took a sleek black leather briefcase from the sideboard.

And then he was gone.

TALLY'S DAY WAS LONG, exhausting—and wonderful.

Her office was a huge, light-filled room, handsomely furnished and perfectly equipped. Selecting an assistant was difficult only because all the candidates Dante's P.A. had chosen were outstanding.

It would have been equally tough to choose one of the nannies but a middle-aged woman with a soft Scottish lilt made things easier when she spotted Sam's photo on Tally's desk and crooned, "Och, the sweet little lamb!"

There was nothing difficult in deciding that Dante's P.A. was the eighth wonder of the world. Joan was fiftyish, elegant, and as warm as she was efficient.

"Just let me know what you need," she said, "and it's as good as yours."

At lunchtime, Tally dashed to Fifth Avenue and did the sort of lightning-fast shopping trip she used to do in the past. Within an hour, she'd bought several trousers, skirts, blazers, cashmere sweaters and a couple of pairs of shoes.

At four, she met with Dante's architect, who showed her the interior changes he was going to make in the new offices. At five, she met with one of her old contacts at the design center. At six, she dismissed Dante's driver and headed for the subway.

Dante would not kiss her anymore, and she would not accept any more favors from him. She was working with him. It was only right that they maintain appropriate behavior.

There was a delay on the subway line. A quarter of an hour passed before the train came and after that, it sat between stations for five endless minutes. When she reached her stop, she went half a block out of her way to buy a chocolate Santa for Sam.

She'd called to talk with her baby half a dozen times and the last time, she'd promised to bring a special treat.

By the time she reached Dante's apartment building,

Tally was feeling wonderful. She was back in the city she loved, involved in a major project, and she'd made peace with the problem of dealing with Dante.

All she had to do was make sure he understood the parameters of their relationship, and—

"Where have you been?"

Dante stood in the entrance to the building, blocking her way. His voice was rough, his face white with unconcealed anger.

"I beg your pardon?"

Mouth set, he clasped her arm and marched her past the doorman to the penthouse elevator.

"I asked you a question. Where the hell were you? You should have been here an hour ago."

She swung toward him, her temper rising to match his as he pushed her, unceremoniously, into the car.

"I should have been here an hour ago?" Tally slapped her hands on her hips. "Are you out of your mind? I don't have to answer to you!"

"You left the office at six. An hour late."

"How nice. You have people spying on me."

"And turned down the use of my car."

"Is your driver a paid informer?"

"And where did you go for lunch? I phoned and you hadn't told Joan or your new assistant where you'd be."

Tally was trembling with anger. "Where I went and why I went there is none of your business. Unless—" The color drained from her face. "Ohmygod, is it Sam? Is my baby ill?"

"No!" Dante stepped in front of her as the car doors opened on his penthouse. "Listen to me. Samantha's fine. This has nothing to do with her."

Sweet relief flooded through her, but it didn't last. She'd accepted a job from this man and moved into his guest suite. If he thought that made her his property, he was wrong.

"Then, get out of my way," she said coldly. "I don't answer to you."

"You damned well will," he said grimly, his hand closing like a steel band around her wrist. "This is New York, not a blip on the map in Vermont. Anything might happen to you on these streets."

"What a short memory you have, Russo!" Tally jerked free of his hand. "I know all about New York. I lived here for five years!"

She had. He knew that. She'd traveled the city's streets, ridden its subways, lived in an apartment alone. Of course he knew that…but things had changed.

He told her so, and she looked at him as if he'd gone crazy.

"Nothing's changed. The city's the same. So am I."

"You're not." His mouth twisted and the ugly suspicions he'd tried to deny while he'd paced the floor and wondered where she was, burst from his lips. "You slept with another man while you belonged to me. How do I know you're not seeing him again?"

Tally's eyes went flat. "You don't," she said coldly, and brushed past him.

Dante let her go. He had to; he was still rational enough to know that if he went after her now, it was a sure bet he'd do something he'd regret.

So he turned his back, strode along the marble floor to the library, flung open the liquor cabinet and poured himself a stiff shot of bourbon. And began pacing again, back and forth on the antique silk carpet before the fireplace, while the hours ticked away.

She'd all but called him crazy.

Hell, maybe she was right.

How come he hadn't thought about this before? All the plans he'd made to bring Tally back to New York and it had never occurred to him that he might be pushing her straight into the arms of her old lover.

The man who'd made her pregnant.

If he wasn't crazy, he was just plain stupid, because the idea hadn't even popped into his head until he'd been at lunch in Philadelphia after a morning of meetings. Somewhere between the salad course and the entrée, he'd suddenly realized he wanted to hear Tally's voice. He'd excused himself, left the table and phoned.

But she wasn't at her office, and Joan had no idea where she'd gone. He'd started to call her on her cell phone, only to realize that he didn't have the number.

He'd gone back to the table. Shoved the grilled shrimps and vegetables back and forth on his plate. Said "yes" and "no" and "how interesting" when it seemed fitting.

And all the while, he'd been thinking, *Where is she? Where did she go?*

That was when he'd first realized that bringing her back to the city might have been a mistake. That even now, while he pretended to pay attention to the details of a billion-dollar deal, Tally might be lying in the arms of the man she'd left him for. She'd slept with the man only once, she'd said, but Tally wasn't like that.

She wouldn't be anybody's one-night stand.

Had she lied about that? Had the bastard been her

lover for weeks? For months? Did she want to go back to him now?

Why would she, when he'd abandoned her when she was pregnant?

He had abandoned her, hadn't he? Because if he hadn't, if something, who the hell knew what, had kept Tally and the SOB apart and that something no longer stood between them—

You are losing your mind, Dante had told himself.

The warning hadn't helped.

Everyone ordered coffee. He lifted his cup, frowned, put it down untouched. He was sorry, he said; he had to leave. And he walked away from three men who stared at him as if they agreed with the silent assessment he'd made of his sanity.

He'd flown back to New York, angry at himself, furious at Tally because it was her fault, all of this, his rage, his distrust, his inability to do anything except think about her. If only she'd never run from him…

Her fault. Entirely.

At home, he'd paced the floor, planning how he'd tell her that if she thought she was going to live with him and take someone else for a lover, she was wrong.

He'd kill the other man before he let that happen.

Then he'd told himself that she wasn't living with him, not in any real sense. Besides, maybe she hadn't gone back to the other man. Maybe she'd told him the truth, that she'd only been with that faceless stranger the one time.

One time had been enough.

The son of a bitch had planted a seed in her womb. He'd given her a child he hadn't helped support, a child who was solely Tally's responsibility. A child who by all rights should have belonged to—should have belonged to—

The clock on the mantel had struck the hour. Seven o'clock. Seven at night, and where the hell was she?

Carlo had no idea. Ms. Sommers had sent his car away. Joan, reached at home, didn't know a thing, either.

And Dante, fueled with a rage he didn't understand, had lost control. He'd paced some more, snarled at his housekeeper when she came in to ask what time he wanted dinner served and, when he was alone again, punched his fist into the wall with such force he was surprised he hadn't put a hole in it.

He went down to the lobby, about to head into the street to find Tally—though he had no idea where in hell he'd start—and saw her come sauntering toward the door, with a smile for the doorman and a blank look for him.

He'd wanted to shake her until her teeth rattled.

He'd wanted to haul her into his arms and kiss her.

In the end, because he knew doing either would be a mistake, he'd launched into a tirade that settled nothing except to prove, once again, he was an idiot where she was concerned.

Dante looked at the clock on the mantel. The hours had raced by. It was two in the morning; the city below was as quiet as it would ever be.

Two in the morning, and he was still ticking like a time bomb while Tally undoubtedly slept peacefully two floors above him.

He tilted the glass to his lips and drained it of bourbon.

Did she get a kick out of this? Out of making him

behave this way? Surely, she knew she had this effect on him.

She did it deliberately.

That was why he'd decided to end their affair three years ago. He hadn't been bored. Who could be bored by a woman who could discuss the stock market and football statistics without missing a beat?

A muscle knotted in his jaw.

He could afford a little honesty now, couldn't he? Admit to himself that the reason he'd wanted to end things was because he'd sensed his feelings for her were becoming uncontrollable?

That night she'd asked him to stay, and he almost had. Other nights when she hadn't asked, when he'd had to force himself from her bed because the thought of leaving her had been agony.

Oh, yes.

Tally was manipulating him. Toying with him and the self-discipline on which he prided himself. The self-discipline that had made him a success.

And he didn't like it, not one bit.

Dante's eyes narrowed. But he knew what to do about it. How to regain that control. Of himself. Of the situation. Of Tally.

Back to Plan A. He would take her to bed.

He had perfect control there. Holding back, not just physically but emotionally. Exulting in what happened between them, feeling it as a hot rush of pleasure so intense he'd never known it with another woman and yet, keeping a little piece of himself from her.

Emotions were not things to put on exhibit. Control was a man's sole protection against a hostile world.

Control, goddamn it, Dante thought.

His hands knotted into fists. Anger burned like a fire in his belly. Anger, and something far more primitive.

Tally was asleep, satisfied she'd made a fool of him again, and he was here, wide awake, trapped like an insect in a web of rage.

"Enough," he growled.

Dante flung open the library door and headed for the stairs.

CHAPTER NINE

MOONLIGHT SPILLED from a sky bright with stars and lay like fine French lace across the floor of Tally's bedroom.

Some other time, she'd have noticed and admired it.

Not tonight.

Instead, she sat curled in a window seat, her back to the night, focused only on the turmoil inside her, anger and pain warring for control of her heart.

She hated Dante, hated the things he'd accused her of. How could he think her capable of being a cheat and a liar?

Maybe because you told him you slept with another man while he was still your lover, a voice inside her whispered contemptuously.

Yes. All right, but what else could she have done? She'd wanted to protect herself and Sam. Now she knew she'd done the right thing. Dante had shown a side of himself she'd never imagined.

She'd always believed he was a man who suppressed his emotions.

Tonight, he'd been a man out of control, capable of anything.

Tally shivered and drew the silk robe more closely around herself. The night seemed endless, especially without Sam in the next room. The baby had dozed off in her play crib in the little room next to the housekeeper's.

"Let her stay the night, Ms. Sommers," Mrs. Tipton had said. "Why wake her from a sound sleep?"

Now Tally was glad she'd left Sam where she was. Her little girl needed the rest. Tomorrow was going to be a busy day.

She and Sam were going home to Shelby.

She'd scrub floors for a living, move into a furnished flat above a storefront on Main Street if she had to. Better that, better to raise her daughter in poverty, than to raise her here.

Tally rose to her feet and paced the bedroom, the details of her confrontation with Dante as alive as if they'd happened minutes instead of hours ago.

What gave him the right to ask where she'd been? To accuse her of sneaking off to be with Samantha's father? She'd come within a breath of laughing in his face at that, except it really wasn't funny.

Okay. She'd made a mistake, accepting this job. Well, a mistake could be remedied. And maybe some good had come of it. At least now she knew exactly what she felt for Dante Russo.

She despised him.

Tally paused, wrapped her arms around herself and drew a shuddering breath. She had to do something or go crazy. She'd pack. Yes. That was an excellent idea. She'd pack now. That way, come morning, all she'd have to do was take Sam and get the hell out of this snake pit.

Ellen had hung all her clothes in the closet, including the things Saks had delivered this afternoon. Tally dumped her old stuff in her suitcase and ignored the rest. Let Dante give it away. Let him burn it, for all she gave a damn.

She didn't want anything his money had bought.

He was a heartless, manipulative, controlling son of a bitch and it made her sick to think she'd ever imagined that she loved him. Anybody could be guilty of a bit of self-deception, but once you knew it you had to do something about it.

She'd spent years in the city, though maybe she was still a small-town girl at heart, unable or unwilling to think she'd slept with a man, borne his child without loving him.

But no woman could love a man who thought he owned you. Who believed you capable of lies and deceit and—

The bedroom door flew open, the sound of it sharp as a gunshot in the quiet night. Tally whirled around.

Dante stood in the doorway, and her heart leaped into her throat.

This was a Dante she'd never seen before.

His suit jacket was gone, as was his tie. His shirt was open at the neck, the sleeves rolled to the elbows, exposing forearms knotted with muscle.

But it was what she saw in the way he held himself that terrified her. The tall, powerful body poised like a big cat's. The dark intensity of his eyes as they fixed on hers. The cruel little smile that tilted across his mouth.

Tally wanted to run but there was nowhere to go. She had to face the enemy.

"What are you doing here, Dante?"

He answered by stepping inside the room and shutting the door behind him.

"It's late," she said.

"I agree. It's very late. I'm here to remedy that."

"And—and Samantha is sleeping. I don't want to wake her."

"Samantha is with Mrs. Tipton." He took another step forward. "Taylor."

He was back to using her given name. How could he make it seem menacing?

"Dante." Her voice quavered. "Dante, please. You want to talk. So do I. But it can wait until morning."

"I don't want to talk, Taylor."

A sob burst from Tally's throat. To hell with facing the enemy. She turned and ran. Sam's bedroom was empty. If she could get there before he reached her—

Two quick steps, and his powerful hands closed on her shoulders; he spun her toward him and she looked up into eyes that glittered with the desolate cold of a polar night.

"No! Don't. Dante—"

He captured her mouth with his, forced her lips apart and penetrated her with his tongue. He tasted of anger and of whiskey, and of a primitive domination that terrified her.

"No," she cried, and struggled to free herself from his grasp, but he laughed, pushed her back against the wall and yanked her hands high above her head.

"Fight me," he growled. "Go on. Fight! It'll make taking you even more pleasurable."

"Please," she panted. "Dante, please. Don't do this. I beg you—"

"All those months I made love to you and it wasn't enough. Is that why you went to him? Did he do things I didn't?"

"Dante. I never—"

He ripped the robe apart, tore her nightgown from the vee between her breasts straight down to her belly.

"Tell me what you wanted that I didn't give you."

"You're wrong. Wrong! It wasn't the way you make it sound. I didn't—"

She cried out as he captured one breast in his hand and rubbed his thumb across the nipple, his cold eyes locked to hers.

"Was it the way he touched your breasts?"

Tears were streaming down her face. Good, he thought. Let her weep. It wouldn't stop him. He would do this. Pierce her flesh with his and banish her from his life, forever.

"Was it the way he touched you here?"

He thrust his hand between her thighs, searching, even in his madness, for the welcoming heat, the sweet moisture he had never forgotten...

And found, instead, the cold, dry flesh of a woman who was unready and unwilling. A woman who was sobbing as if her heart were breaking...

As she had broken his.

Dante went still. He looked at Tally's face and felt the coldness inside him melting.

"Tally."

His arms went around her; he gathered her to him, his hands stroking her back, her hair. He kissed her forehead, her wet eyes, and as she wept he whispered to her, soft words in his native language, but she stood rigid within his embrace, still quietly crying as if the world were about to end.

"Tally." Dante framed her face between his hands. "*Inamorata*. Forgive me. Please. Don't cry. I won't hurt you. I could never hurt you." He raised her chin, looked into her eyes and saw a darkness and despair that chilled his soul.

He dragged in a deep breath, hating himself, hating what he had almost done, knowing that what was driving him was not hate or anger but something else. Something foreign to his life and to him.

A fear he'd never known gripped him.

He'd fought toughs on the streets of Palermo. Faced down CEOs in hostile boardrooms. Made believers of financial analysts who'd looked him in the eye and assured him he couldn't do any of the things he'd ended up doing.

He was a warrior. Each battle he survived made him stronger.

But he wasn't a warrior now. He was a man, holding in his arms a woman he'd already lost once before. She had run from him and he knew, in his heart of hearts, that she'd run because he had somehow failed her.

She'd turned to another man for the same reason.

If she ran again, if he lost her again…

"Tally."

He held her closer. Rained kisses over her hair. Said her name over and over, and finally, finally when he'd almost given up hope, she lifted her face to his.

"I wasn't with anyone," she whispered. "I never wanted anyone but you, Dante. Never. Never. Nev—"

He kissed her. With all his heart, his soul, with all he had ever been or ever hoped to be, and Tally wound her arms around his neck and kissed him back. They had kissed a thousand times. A million times...but never like this, as if their lives hung in the balance.

Mouths fused, Dante swept Tally into his arms and carried her to the bed.

At first, it was enough. The taste of her mouth. The warmth of his breath. Her sighs. His whispers. The stroke of her hand on his face, of his hand on her throat...

It was enough.

Inevitably, it changed.

Dante could feel the tension growing inside him. The need to take more. To give more. To suck Tally's nipples, put his mouth between her thighs and inhale her exquisite scent.

It was the same for Tally. She needed Dante's mouth on her flesh. His hands on her breasts. Needed to lift her hips to him, impale herself on his rock-hard erection so that she could fly with him to the stars.

"Dante," she whispered.

Everything a man could dream was in the way she spoke his name.

He eased the robe and tattered nightgown from her shoulders, kissing the hollow in her throat, the delicate skin over her collarbone.

She was lovely. As beautiful as he'd remembered.

There was a new fullness to her breasts now. The child, Dante thought, and felt a swift pain at the realization that someone else had given that child to her, but it left him quickly because there was so much more to the woman in his arms than that one moment of infidelity.

He bent his head, kissed the slope of each breast. Brushed a finger lightly over a pale-pink nipple.

Watched her face as he played the nub of flesh delicately between thumb and forefinger, and felt the fierce tightening low in his belly when she sobbed his name as he drew the nub into his mouth.

She tasted like cream and honey; she tasted like the Tally he'd never forgotten, never wanted to forget, and when she tugged impatiently at his shirt he sat up, tried unbuttoning it, cursed and tore it off. Peeled off the rest of his clothing and took her in his arms again.

The hot feel of her breasts against his chest almost undid him. Dante groaned, clenched his teeth, warned himself to hang onto his control.

But she was moving beneath him, rubbing herself against his engorged flesh. She was slick and hot, and the exciting scent of her arousal was more precious to him than all the perfumes in the world.

"Please," she said, kissing his shoulder. "Please, please, please…"

"Soon," he whispered, but she arched against him and he was lost. Nothing mattered but this. This, he thought, and entered her on one long, hard thrust.

Tally screamed. Her hands dug into his hair; she wrapped her legs around his hips and bit his shoulder and he let go. Of himself, of his past, of the restraints that had always defined his life.

Together, they soared over the edge of the earth, two hearts, two souls, two bodies merged as one.

AFTERWARD, they lay in each other's arms and shared soft kisses. They touched and sighed, and then Tally's breathing slowed.

"Go to sleep, *inamorata*," Dante whispered.

"What does that mean? *Inamorata?*"

He kissed her. "It means beloved."

Tally smiled and he kissed her again.

"Go to sleep."

"I'm not sleepy," she murmured.

And slept.

Dante gathered her closer against him. How had he endured three long years without this woman in his life?

Except, he had never really let her into his life. They'd been lovers for six months back then but he'd kept his distance. He always did. Dinners out at the city's best restaurants instead of pasta and vino by the fire. Center row seats at the newest Broadway show instead of an evening of old movies on the DVD. Dancing at the latest club instead of swaying in each other's arms to a Billy Joel CD.

How come?

And how come he didn't even know if she liked old movies? If she liked Billy Joel or maybe newer stuff?

Because he'd never let her into his life. That was how come. It was the same reason he'd called her Taylor, when any fool could see that under all the urban glamour, she was really a girl named Tally.

And he—and he felt something special for her.

His arms tightened around her. He wanted to make love to her again but she was sleeping so soundly…

Okay. He'd kiss her closed eyes. Gently. Like that. Kiss her mouth. Tenderly. Yes, that way. Kiss it again and if she sighed, as she was sighing now, if her lips parted so that he could taste her sweetness, yes, like that… If her lashes fluttered and she looked up at him and smiled and linked her hands behind his neck the way she was doing now, would it be wrong to kiss her again? To run his hand gently down her body? To groan as she lifted herself to him, cradled his body between her thighs?

"Make love to me," Tally whispered.

And he would. He would—but first, he lifted her in his arms and rose from the bed.

"Where are we going?"

"To my room," he said huskily. "To my bed. It's where you belong, *inamorata,* where you always should have been." He kissed her. "Where you will be, from this night on."

HIS ROOM WAS SHADOWED, his bed high and wide.

They made love again, slowly, tenderly, until passion swept them up and Dante brought Tally down on him, impaled her on him, and watched her face as she rode him to fulfillment. They slept in each other's arms and awakened again at dawn, Tally wordlessly drawing Dante to her, sighing his name against his throat as he rocked into her and took her with him to the stars.

When she awoke next, it was to the kiss of the morning sun. Dante lay next to her, head propped on his fist, watching her with a soft smile on his lips.

Tally smiled, too. "Hello," she whispered.

He leaned over and kissed her mouth. "Hello, *bellissima.*"

She stretched with lazy abandon. The sheet dropped to her waist. Dante seized the moment and kissed her breasts.

"Sweet," he murmured.

She smiled again. She might never stop smiling, she thought, clasping his face between her hands and pressing a light kiss to his lips.

"I love it when you kiss me," he said softly.

She loved it, too. She could spend the morning like this, just kissing, touching, locked away from reality....

Oh, God. Locked away from Samantha.

"Tally. What's wrong?"

Everything, Tally thought, and it was all her fault. She moved out of Dante's arms and sat up, suddenly conscious of her nudity.

Dante sat up, too, and caught her in his arms. "Talk to me. What's the matter?"

"Sam's an early riser."

"Is that what's worrying you?" Smiling, he drew her to him. "So is Mrs. Tipton."

"Sam is my daughter. My responsibility. Not your housekeeper's."

"Damn it, Tally, don't look away from me." He clasped her face, forced her eyes to meet his. "Moments ago you were in my arms. Now you're looking at me as if we're strangers. Talk to me. Tell me what you're thinking."

Tell him what? That the long, wonderful night had been a mistake? Because it had been. Yes, he'd brought her to his bed, but nothing had changed. She loved him. Why lie to herself? She loved him, she always would...

And all he felt for her was desire.

It hadn't been enough three years ago. It was why she'd decided to leave him, even before she'd known she was carrying his baby. She'd loved him so much that hearing him say he'd tired of her would have killed her.

Now she'd put herself in the same position. He wanted her because she'd defied him, but the novelty would wear thin. He'd tire of her as he had in the past and they'd be right back where they started, with one enormous difference.

This time, she wouldn't be the only one who'd pay the price for her foolishness.

Samantha would pay, as well.

Her daughter. Dante's daughter. God, oh God, oh God…

"Tally?"

She pulled free of his embrace, plucked his robe from the chair beside the bed and slipped it on.

"Dante." Tally got to her feet. "This was—it was a mistake."

He sat up, the comforter dropping to his waist. "What are you talking about?" he said, his voice sharp.

"I shouldn't have slept with you." She tried not to look at him as he rose from the bed, naked and beautifully masculine. "I—I enjoyed last night." The look on his face made her take a quick step back. "But it shouldn't have happened. I have a daughter. That makes everything different. I can't just live for the moment anymore, I have to think of her. Of how much what I do affects her."

"You're a fine mother, *bellissima*. Anyone can see that."

"I try to be. And that means I can't—I can't sleep with you and then go about my life as if nothing's happened. I can't—" Tally caught her breath as he reached for her. "You're not listening."

"I am," he said softly. Gently, he brushed his lips over hers. "You don't want your little girl to see her mother take a lover."

"That's part of it."

"To live a life with her, and a separate one with him."

Tally nodded. He was more perceptive than she'd given him credit for. "She won't understand. And I can't do something that will confuse her. Do you see?"

"Better than you think, *cara*." He hesitated. "I only wish my own mother had thought the same way."

The words were simple but they caught her by surprise. He had never mentioned anything about his past before.

"She took lover after lover," he said, his mouth twisting, "if that's what you want to call them. Sometimes she brought them home. 'This is Guiseppe,' she'd say. Or Angelo or Giovanni or whoever he was, the man of the hour. Then she'd tell me to be a good boy and go out and play."

"Oh, Dante. That must have been—"

"When I was six, seven—I'm not certain. All I know is that one day, she took me to my *nonna's*—my grandmother's. 'Be a good boy, Dante,' she said. And—"

"And?" Tally said softly.

He shrugged. "And I never saw her again."

Tally wanted to take him in her arms and hold him close, but she didn't. She sensed that the moment was fragile, that it would take little to tear it apart.

"I'm sorry," she said quietly. "That must have been—it must have been hard."

Another shrug, as if it didn't matter, but when he spoke, the tension in his voice told her that it did.

"I survived."

"And grew into a strong, wonderful man."

Dante looked at her. "Not so wonderful," he said, "or you wouldn't have left me three years ago."

This time, she did reach out, even if it was only to touch her hand to his cheek.

"I grew up living with my grandmother, too," she said quietly.

"In that little house in Vermont?"

She nodded. "My mother was—Grandma called her flighty." She managed a quick smile. "What it really means is that she took off when I was little and never came back. My father had already done the same thing, even before I was born."

Dante gathered her into his arms.

"What a pair we make," he said gently.

Tally nodded again. "All the more reason that I can't—why we can't—"

"Yes. I agree," he murmured, tucking a strand of hair behind her ear, "and I have the perfect solution."

"There is no solution. I have to protect Sam." *Sam and me.*

"Of course there is." Dante tilted her face to his. "You'll move out of the guest suite."

One night? Was that all he'd wanted? Tally forced herself to nod in agreement.

"Of course. I'll find an apartment and—"

"And," he said softly, "you'll move in with me. We'll let Sam see that we are—that we are together. That we are part of each other's lives, and that she is, too."

Tally stared at him, her face a mask of confusion. Was she trying to find a way to tell him she wouldn't go along with his plan? It had come to him during the night; he'd been pleased with it until this moment, when he realized that Tally might not want to be with him this way.

"Tally." His hands slid to her shoulders. "Please." His fingers bit into her flesh. "Tell me want to be with me. I don't want to lose you again. Say yes."

Her head whispered of reservations, of questions, of why the arrangement would never work...

But Tally listened to her heart and said, "Yes."

CHAPTER TEN

THROUGHOUT THE AGES, wise men caution that a man who makes decisions in the heat of the moment might very well live to regret them.

Dante had always agreed.

He was not impulsive. He made choices only after he had examined all the facts. If a man did anything less, he might, indeed, live to regret his decisions.

And yet, he'd acted on impulse when he'd asked Tally to live with him.

It should have been a mistake. The worst mistake of his life, considering that he'd never asked a woman to do that before. Living together, spending your days and nights with one woman, was the kind of involvement he'd always avoided. He liked to come and go as he pleased, to spend time in a woman's company only when he was in the mood.

Add a small child to the mix and a man would surely go crazy.

At least, that was what he'd have said of this new arrangement a week ago. A disaster in the making, he'd have called it…

Dante smiled as he stood at his office window and watched the lights wink on over Manhattan.

He'd have been wrong.

Asking Tally to live with him had turned out to be the best decision he'd ever made. Being with her, with Samantha, had already changed his life.

He'd lived in New York for more than a dozen years and most of that time he'd lived very comfortably. As his fortune grew, he'd become accustomed to a certain start and finish to his day.

In the morning, his housekeeper would ask if he'd be home for dinner; in the evening, she'd inquire pleasantly as to how his day had gone. If the doorman made a comment beyond "Good morning" or "Good evening" it was about the weather. His driver might exchange a few polite words with him about European soccer or American football.

Dante's smile became a grin. How that had changed!

Mrs. Tipton regaled him with stories about Sam. Carlo, whose grandson turned out to be Sam's age, was a font of helpful advice. Even the doorman got into the act with details of Sam's latest adventure among the big potted plants in the lobby.

Sam herself, a bundle of energy with big green eyes and a toothy grin, started and ended his days with sloppy kisses.

Amazing, all of it.

But most amazing was his Tally, who fell asleep in his arms each night and awoke in them each morning. She was the most incredible woman he'd ever known, and he wasn't the only one who thought so.

His architect told him she had the best eye for detail

he'd ever seen. His contractor said she made suggestions that were as innovative as they were practical. Even his P.A., a woman who had seen everything and was surprised by nothing, called her remarkable.

His household staff flat-out adored her.

But not as much as he did.

Dante tucked his hands in his trouser pockets and rocked back on his heels. He'd never believed in luck. What you got out of life was in direct proportion to what you put into it, and yet he knew it was luck, good fortune, whatever you wanted to call it, that had given him this second chance with Tally.

He'd lost her through his own callous behavior. He understood that now. He'd treated her like a possession, taking her from the shelf when he wanted to show her off, returning her when he'd finished. It was how he'd always treated his lovers. Kept them at a distance, bought them elaborate gifts, and politely eliminated them from his life when he got bored.

Dante's jaw clenched.

But Tally had never behaved like his other lovers. She'd kept herself at a distance. That was why she'd refused his elaborate gifts and left behind the ones he'd insisted she accept. And she had never bored him. Never. Not for a moment, in bed or out.

At some point, he'd realized it. And it had shaken him to the core. He'd reacted by pushing her away because he hadn't been ready to admit what she had come to mean to him. As recently as a few weeks ago, he'd still been lying to himself about his feelings for her.

That whole thing about wanting to sleep with her to get revenge, get her out of his system…

Sheer, unadulterated idiocy.

It had always been easier to pretend she was just another woman passing through his life than admit his Tally was special. That what he felt for her was special. That what he felt for her was—that it was—

"Dante?"

He swung around, saw her in the doorway and felt his heart swell. And when she smiled, he thought it might burst.

"I knocked," she said, with a little smile, "but you didn't—"

Dante held out his arms. She went into them and he held her close.

"You look beautiful," he said softly.

She leaned back in his embrace. "Not too dressed up?"

He shook his head. "Perfect."

That was the only word to describe her in a softly clinging silk dress and matching jacket in a color he'd have called green but he suspected women gave a more complex name. Her shoes were wispy things, all straps and slender heels, the kind that made a man imagine his woman wearing them with whatever was under the dress and nothing else.

Dante had a pretty good idea of what was under that dress. He'd bought Tally a drawer full of wispy lingerie from The Silk Butterfly, a shop he'd passed on Fifth Avenue.

"Hand-sewn lace," she'd said, her cheeks taking on a light blush. "I'll feel naked under my clothes." And he'd taken her in his arms and shown her just how exciting that would be for them both.

"I know tonight's important to you."

"You're what's important to me."

"Yes, but tonight—the Children's Fund dinner…"

"Tally. We don't have to go. I told you that. We can have a quiet dinner at that little place on the corner and—"

"No. No, I don't want you to change anything because of me. Everyone you know will be there."

"Everyone *we* know. And they'll see how happy we are to be together again."

She nodded, but her eyes were clouded. "There'll be questions."

Dante raised one eyebrow. "No one will dare to ask questions of me." That made her laugh, just as he'd hoped it would. He took her hand, brought it to his mouth and kissed it. "I missed you."

"You saw me an hour ago," she said with another little laugh.

"And that's far too long to be without you." He drew her closer. "It's going to cost you a kiss."

"Dante. Someone will see."

"I don't care."

"But—"

"If I don't get a kiss from you this very minute," he said dramatically, "my death will be on your hands."

She laughed again. He loved the sound of her laugh, the way her lips curved into an eminently kissable bow. He loved everything about her.

The truth was, he loved—he loved—

Dante bent his head and kissed her.

THEY ARRIVED a few minutes late and found five of their dinner companions already at the table. A well-known real estate agent and his third trophy wife. Dennis and Eve. A used-car salesman turned self-help guru, whose latest feel-good book had just gone into its fifth printing.

Tally remembered them all.

And, clearly, they remembered her. She could almost hear their jaws hit the table when they saw her.

Dante had his arm firmly around her waist.

"Good evening," he said pleasantly. "Tally, I think you know everyone here, don't you?"

"Yes," she said brightly, "of course. How are you, Lila? Donald? Eve and Dennis, how good to see you again. And Mark. Your newest book just came out, didn't it? I hope it's doing well?"

Dante pulled out her chair, whispered, "Good girl," as she slipped into it. He sat down beside her, took her hand and held it in his, right on the tabletop where everyone could see. Five pairs of eyes took in the sight. Then someone said, "Well, I see we're going to have chicken for the main course. Surprise, surprise."

Everyone laughed, and that broke the ice.

People began chatting. Wasn't the weather particularly cold for December? Was snow in the forecast again? Wasn't the ballroom handsomely decorated?

I might just get through this, Tally thought…

"DanteDarling," a woman screeched.

And Tally looked up, inhaled a cloud of obscenely expensive perfume, saw Charlotte LeBlanc swoop down to plant a kiss on Dante's mouth even as he jerked back in his chair, saw the woman's hate-filled gaze fix on her before she switched it to a big, artificial smile…

And knew, instinctively, that Charlotte LeBlanc had, probably until very recently, been Dante's mistress.

"Taylor," Charlotte said. "What a surprise!"

"Yes," Tally said, "yes, I—I suppose it is."

"A wonderful surprise," Dante said, squeezing Tally's hand, but he was looking at Charlotte, his eyes cold with warning, and any doubts Tally might have had about her lover's relationship with the LeBlanc woman vanished.

Conversation swirled around her, the polite stuff people discussed when they were casual acquaintances. Eve talked about her new hair stylist. Dennis said he was buying a new yacht. The self-help guru was also buying one. The real estate agent was too busy eating his shrimp cocktail to say anything. His trophy wife was silent, too, perhaps because her face was frozen in Botoxed bliss.

And suddenly, in a lull in the chatter, Charlotte leaned over, her breasts almost spilling from her neckline, and laid a taloned hand on Tally's arm.

"Taylor," she cooed, "you must tell us all where you've been the last few years."

"She's been in New England," Dante said smoothly. "Building a successful business."

"New England. How quaint." Her smile glittered with malice. "And are you here on business?"

"Taylor's working on a project of mine."

"How nice." Her head swiveled toward Dante. "And you, DanteDarling. Are you and I still on for Christmas in Aspen?"

Dante's eyes went black. "No," he said coldly, "we are not. I told you that weeks ago,"

"Oh, but everyone knows how you tend to change your mind, DanteDarling. How fickle you are, well, not about business but about, you know, other things."

There was no mistaking what "things" she meant. Heads swiveled from Charlotte to Tally to Dante, who snarled a word no one had to speak Sicilian to comprehend.

Charlotte turned red. Everyone else gasped. And Tally pushed her chair back from the table.

"Tally! Damn it, Tally…"

Luck was with her. The band was playing and the dance floor was crowded with couples. Tally wove through the mob, pulled open the door to the ladies' room and slammed it behind her. A sob burst from her throat.

How could she have been so stupid? He'd been with that woman. With Charlotte. He'd been with God only knew how many women these last three years. She'd dreamed of him, yearned for him, wanted only him despite all the lies she'd told herself, but Dante…

"Tally!"

His fist slammed against the door.

"Tally! Open this door or I'm coming in."

One of the stall doors swung open. A woman stepped out and stared at her.

"Tally, do you hear me? Open this goddamned door!"

Tally went to the sink, splashed cold water on her face. She would have ignored the hammering on the door but the woman who'd come out of the stall was looking at her as if she'd somehow wandered into the sort of situation that ended in bloodshed.

There was nothing for it but to square her shoulders and walk out of the ladies' room, straight into a muscled wall of male fury.

"Dante," she said quietly, "please, step aside."

He answered by clasping her shoulders and hauling her to her toes.

"If I'd known that bitch would be at our table," he demanded, "do you really think I'd have brought you here tonight?"

"It doesn't matter. Step aside, please."

"Of course it matters! Damn it, she means nothing to me!"

"Dante. Get out of my—"

"Are you deaf?" His hands bit hard into her flesh as he lowered his face to hers. "She doesn't matter."

"She matters enough so you were going to take her to Aspen."

"She suggested it. I said no. In fact, I never saw her after that evening. We were finished and she knew it."

Tally looked into his eyes. They were the color of smoke, and without warning, the pain inside her burst free.

"You slept with her," she whispered.

His mouth twisted. "Tally. *Bellissima...*"

"You should have told me. So I—I could have been prepared to see the way she looked at you. To know you'd been with her, made love to her—"

"It was sex," he said roughly. "Only sex. Never anything more."

She stared into his eyes again. *And what is it with me?* she longed to say, but her heart knew better than to ask.

"How many were there?" Her voice trembled and she hated herself for it. She'd known a man virile as Dante wouldn't live like a monk but to see the proof for herself... "How many women after me?"

His grasp on her tightened. "What does it matter? All

the years we were apart, I never stopped thinking of you. I hated you for leaving me, Tally—and hated myself for not being able to get over you."

Tally looked away from him, certain that her heart was going to break. If he couldn't get over her, how could he have betrayed her with other women? In the endless years since leaving him, she had never even thought of anyone else. She had never betrayed him...

But she had.

Running away had been a kind of betrayal. Even the cold, cleverly worded note she'd left had been a betrayal.

And then there was the cruelest betrayal of all. She'd told him she'd cheated on him with another man, that she'd given birth to that man's child.

"Tally." His voice was thick with anguish. "There's never been anyone but you. You must believe me!"

Slowly she lifted her eyes to his. "What I believe," she whispered, "is that we've both been fools."

He nodded. She could see color returning to his face.

"Yes. We have been, but we won't be any longer." He framed her face with his hands and raised it to his. "I'm not going to lose you again, *inamorata*. I won't let it happen."

Tears gathered on Tally's lashes. Gently Dante kissed them away. Then he wrapped his arm around her shoulders.

"Let's go home."

She smiled. "Yes. Let's go home."

He led her past the curious little group that had been watching them, out of the hotel and into his waiting limousine. Part of him wanted to go back to the ballroom, put his hands around Charlotte's throat and make her pay for what she'd done.

But he was every bit as guilty.

Not for having slept with Charlotte. Tally had been out of his life then. Not even for having not told her about Charlotte. He was a man, not a saint. What man would deliberately tell the woman he cared for that he'd slept with someone else, even if he'd been absolutely free to do so at the time?

He pressed a kiss to Tally's hair as she sat curled against him, her head on his shoulder.

His guilt was over what he'd done three years ago.

He'd let Tally slip away. And he should have gone after her. Should have faced what she meant to him because the truth was he didn't just care for her, he—he—

"Dante?"

Dante cleared his throat. "Yes, *cara?*"

"I'm sorry."

"No! It wasn't your fault."

"Not about tonight. I'm… I'm sorry for…for—" She took a deep breath and sat up straight, her eyes locked to his. "We need to talk. But not here. Someplace… someplace where we can be alone."

Suddenly he knew that was what he wanted, too. A quiet place where they could be alone. Where they could talk—and he could finally confront what was in his heart.

"I have an idea," he said slowly. "Christmas is next week. What if we spend it alone? Just the three of us. You and me and Samantha. We'll go somewhere warm, where we can lie in the sun in each other's arms, where Sam can run around to her heart's content. Would you like that?"

"A place where we can talk," Tally said softly.

Talk about what had really made her run away, she thought as Dante drew her against him, because tonight, she'd finally faced the truth.

No matter what happened, she had to tell Dante that she loved him.

That there'd never been another man.

That he was Sam's father.

CHAPTER ELEVEN

WHAT COULD BE more wonderful than lying in the curve of your lover's arm on a white sand beach under the hot Caribbean sun?

Tally turned her head and put her mouth lightly against Dante's bronzed skin, savoring the exciting taste of salt and man.

How she adored him!

Her Dante was everything a man should be. Strong. Tender. Giving. Demanding. Fiercely passionate, incredibly gentle. She loved him, loved him, loved him...

And it killed her that she'd lied to him.

That she was still lying to him, because she'd yet to tell him the truth about Sam.

Soon, she thought, as she closed her eyes and burrowed closer to his warm, hard body. She'd confess everything to him this evening, after dinner, when they were both tucking Sam in for the night. Or tomorrow morning, at breakfast. And if the time didn't seem right then, she'd wait just another few hours. Another few days...

Tally swallowed hard. *Liar,* she thought, *liar, liar, liar!*

She wouldn't tell him tonight, or tomorrow. Or ever,

at the rate she was going. She wanted to. Wanted to say, *Dante, I've done an awful thing. I lied to you about Sam. About being with someone else. Sam is your child. Ever since we met, there's only been you.*

The problem was, she could see beyond that.

She had let him think she'd been unfaithful.

She had denied him knowledge of his own child.

Who could predict how he'd react?

Some days, she was sure he would understand. Others, she was afraid he wouldn't. She'd thought it would be so easy to admit everything once they were here, on this beautiful island in the midst of a sea as clear as fine green glass, tucked away from the world in a magnificent house on its own long, pristine, private beach. Just the three of them: she and Dante and Samantha. No housekeeper. No maid. No nanny or chauffeur. Just she and the man she loved and her little girl.

Their little girl.

Except, Dante didn't know that yet because she was a coward, because she was terrified of what he'd say, what he'd do when he knew she'd deceived him in the worst way possible—

"*Bellissima,* what's wrong?" Tally's eyes flew open as Dante brushed his lips over hers. "You were whimpering in your sleep, *cara.* Were you having a bad dream?"

"I… I… Yes. Something like that."

Smiling, he kissed her again. "You've been in the sun too long. That's the problem."

Now. Tell him now!

"Dante."

"Hmm?" He bent to her and kissed her again, parting

her lips and slowly slipping the tip of his tongue into her mouth. "You taste delicious."

So did he. Oh, so did—

"Dante." Her breath caught. His mouth was at her throat, her breast, nipping lightly at the rapidly beading tip through the thin cotton of her bikini top. "Dante…"

"I'll bet you taste even more delicious here," he whispered as he slid his hands behind her, undid the top, his eyes shining brightest silver as he exposed her breasts. "Let me see if I'm right."

Tally cried out, arching against him as he drew her nipple into the wet heat of his mouth; even as he began easing her bikini bottom down her thighs, she felt it starting to happen, the shimmering heat building inside her, the hot rush of desire as he stroked her dampening curls, put his mouth to her until she was begging him, pleading with him, to take her.

Slowly, so slowly that she thought it might never end, prayed it might never end, he entered her. Filled her, stretched her, moved deep inside her while he whispered to her in Sicilian, words she didn't know but somehow understood, and she thought, *I love you, Dante. I've always loved you. Only you.*

And shattered like crystal in his arms.

AFTER, HE CARRIED HER into the house, past the room where Samantha lay sleeping, to their bedroom and their canopied bed overlooking the sea.

Gently, he lay her in the center of the white sheets, came down beside her and drew her into his arms. Tally put her face in his neck and sighed.

"I love it here," she said softly.

"I'm glad."

"The house is so beautiful. And the sea... I've never seen a sea this clear."

Dante smiled as he stroked his hand gently up and down her spine. "There's a beach on the Mediterranean where you can stand knee-deep in the water and watch tiny fish swim by like flashes of blue and green light."

Tally tilted her head back so she could see his face. "Is that where you lived with your *nonna?* In a town by the sea?"

"Nothing so postcard-perfect, *cara.* I grew up in Palermo, on a street that was already old when Rome ruled the world."

"It sounds wonderful. All that history—"

"Trust me, Tally. There was nothing wonderful about it. Everyone was dirt-poor, except for us." He gave a self-deprecating laugh. "We were poorer than that."

"Then, everything you have today—you built it all, from scratch?" She smiled. "The amazing Mr. Russo."

He grinned, lifted her so that she lay stretched out along his length.

Well," he said, "if you want to call me that—"

Tally rolled her eyes, brought her mouth to his and kissed him. "Don't let it go to your head," she said softly, "but you really are. Amazing."

Dante framed her face with his hands. "What's amazing," he whispered, "is you."

That brought her back to reality. "Dante," she said carefully, "Dante, do you remember what I said the other night? That we have to talk."

"I agree. We do." His eyes grew hooded. "But not right now."

"Dante. Please—"

"Please what?" He cupped her hips, eased her to her knees above him. "Please, this?" he whispered, and she felt the tip of his erection kiss her labia. "Tell me and I'll do it. I'll do whatever you want, *inamorata*. Anything. Everything…"

Then he was inside her, and words had no meaning. All that mattered was this. This…

This.

AN HOUR LATER, Dante eased his arm from beneath Tally's shoulders, touched his mouth lightly to hers, slipped on a pair of denim shorts and went to check on Sam.

The baby woke just as he peeked into her room. When she saw him, she grinned, said "Da-Tay" and held out her chubby arms. Dante grinned back, picked her up and gave her a kiss.

"Hello, *bambina*. Did you have a good nap?"

"Goo'nap," she said happily.

"I'll bet you need a diaper change."

"Di-chain," Sam gurgled, and Dante laughed.

"You're a regular little echo chamber, aren't you?"

"Eck-chame," Sam said.

Dante laughed again, put her on the changing table and replaced her wet diaper with a fresh one. Then he carried her through the house, into the kitchen, put her in the booster chair at the table while he filled a sippy-cup with milk. She liked it warm so he heated it in the microwave oven, tested a drop on his wrist, screwed the top on, plucked her from the booster, went out on the porch and sat down with her in his arms.

She could handle the sippy-cup herself and he knew

it, but he liked holding her, liked the warm weight of the baby, her sweet smell, the little noises of delight she made as she fed.

He liked caring for Samantha in general. Well, maybe not the poopy-diapers part, which he'd done when he heard her babbling softly to herself early this morning. Why wake Tally when he could change the diaper himself, even if it had been a rather interesting learning experience?

The truth was, he'd never imagined himself with a baby in his arms. Oh, he'd figured on having children someday. A man wanted children to carry on his genes, his life's work, but his thoughts had been of faceless miniature adults and a faceless perfect wife. Now, of course, he knew better.

He wanted a little girl exactly like Sam.

A wife exactly like Tally.

Dante caught his breath.

And, just that easily, came face-to-face with the truth.

He loved Tally. He loved her daughter. He had his family already, right here, the baby in his arms, the woman he adored in his bed.

He rose to his feet, ready to rush to the bedroom, wake Tally with a kiss, tell her what was in his heart—

No. He wanted this to be just right. All the romantic touches he'd always scoffed at. Candlelight. Flowers. Champagne.

The travel agent had given him the name of a respected island family that lived nearby. He waited until Sam finished her milk. Then he kept her safely in the curve of his arm while he made some phone calls. When he was done, he'd arranged for a babysitter, reserved a secluded table at a five-star restaurant on the beach, and ordered a ten-carat canary-yellow diamond in a platinum setting from the delighted owner of the island's most exclusive jewelry shop, with instructions to have a messenger bring the ring to the restaurant promptly at nine that night.

He was about to order flowers when Sam giggled and said, "Mama!"

Dante looked up and saw Tally.

"Hey," she said, smiling.

"Hey," he said softly, smiling back at her.

"You should have woken me."

"Your hear that, kid? Your mother doesn't think we can handle the tough stuff on our own." He paused. "Tally?"

"Hmm?"

I love you. I adore you. I want to marry you and adopt Sam, raise her as our very own daughter...

"What on earth are you thinking" she said, with a little laugh. "You have the strangest look on your face!"

"Do I?" He cleared his throat. "Maybe it's because—because what I was thinking was that I want to celebrate Christmas this evening."

Tally laughed. "Christmas is two days away!"

"You don't think I'm going to permit a little detail like that to stop me, do you?" Smiling, he came toward her. Sam held out her arms and he handed her to her mother. "In fact, I've already made plans for us tonight."

"What plans?" Tally said, hugging her daughter, putting her face up for Dante's kiss, thinking how right all this was, being here together, the man she loved, the child they'd created together. "What plans?" she said again and knew that tonight, no matter what happened, she would tell him everything.

His smile tilted. "It's a surprise. A good one," he added softly, "one I hope will make you happy." He put his arms around them both, the woman he loved and the child he would make his.

The child that should have been his, if he hadn't been so stupid and self-involved.

He felt the dull pain of regret settle over him.

If only Sam really were his. He loved her but some-times—sometimes it hurt to know that Tally had lain with another man. That someone else had joined with her to create this beautiful little life.

"Dante," Tally said softly, "what's wrong?"

"Nothing." He cleared his throat. "I was just thinking about tonight."

"You looked—you looked sad."

"Sad?" He smiled, forced the dark thoughts away. "Nonsense," he said briskly. "I'm just making sure I've thought of everything. Sam's babysitter. Our dinner res-ervations."

"Are we having dinner out?"

"We are. At that place on the beach."

Tally gave him the look women have always given men who are too dense to understand life's basic rules of survival.

"That place? But I don't have anything to wear! You said we'd only need swimsuits. Shorts. Jeans. I can't go there in jeans, Dante!"

He thought she could go there in what she wore now and still be more beautiful than any woman in the place, but this played right into his hands. He still had things to arrange. The flowers for their meal and for the house when they returned to it later. Candles for the bedroom.

More champagne, to drink on the beach once she had his ring on her finger.

"I agree," he said solemnly. "That's why you're going to take my credit card, taxi into town and buy whatever you need for tonight."

"But—"

He silenced the protest with a kiss.

"Find something long and elegant. Something so sexy it will make every man who sees you want me dead so he can claim you for his own." He kissed her again and she leaned into him, the baby gurgling happily between them, and half an hour later, holding Sam in his arms, both of them waving as the taxi and Tally pulled away, Dante knew he was, without question, the luckiest man alive.

HE MADE THE BALANCE of the phone calls, arranged for the delivery of white orchids, white candles and bottles of Cristal. The last call went to his attorney in New York, where he left a message asking him to research the state's adoption laws and to determine the quickest way to effect an adoption.

"I think that about does it, Sammy," he said, grinning at the way Samantha looked when he called her that. It wasn't elegant, but he liked it.

Then he turned all his attention on the child who would soon be his.

He took her into the pool, rode her on his shoulders in the warm water as she laughed and clutched at his hair with her fists.

He held her hand as they walked along the beach, helping her pick up shells, making a show of putting them into his pocket for later while surreptitiously letting ones that were too small for her safety fall to the sand.

He made himself a cup of coffee, handed Sam a sippy-cup of juice and shared an Oreo cookie with her, chuckling as he imagined what all those who trembled at his presence in a boardroom would think if they could see him eating the chunks she handed him, baby drool and all.

Late afternoon, with the sun high overhead, he sat on the palm-shaded patio, Sam playing at his feet. She gave a huge yawn.

"Nap time," he said.

Sam, who was, of course, brilliant for her age, puckered up her baby face and yowled.

"Okay, okay, forget I mentioned it."

The baby smiled, yawned again, put her head down and her rump up, and promptly fell asleep on the blanket at his feet. Dante yawned, too, picked up the magazine he'd been leafing through, wondered if Tally—his Tally—would be as happy as he wanted her to be when he proposed tonight.

She would—wouldn't she?

She loved him—didn't she?

He hadn't really thought about it until now. Yes. Of course she loved him. The way she sighed in his arms. Smiled into his eyes. The way he caught her watching him sometimes, that little smile curving her lips—

What was that? A dark shape, near his foot.

"Dio mio!"

Sam woke up screaming as a thing with eight legs raced across her outflung hand. Dante scooped the child into his arms, stomped on the ugly black thing and saw the bite marks of its fangs on Sam's tender wrist.

"Sam," he said, "Sam, *mia figlia*—"

Her shriek of pain rose into the air. Even as he scooped her into his arms, Dante saw the flesh around the bite start to swell. He paused only long enough to tie a scarf around her arm above the bite and to pick up the dead spider, place it in his handkerchief and tuck it into his pocket.

Heart racing, he ran for his car.

HE PHONED THE HOSPITAL when he was two blocks away. Two physicians and a nurse were waiting outside the emergency room. The nurse tried to take Sam from his arms but he refused to give her up.

"I'm staying with her," he said, and neither the doctors nor the nurse doubted his determination.

They led him into an examining room. Sam clung to his neck, sobbing. He soothed her with words he barely knew, things he'd heard people say to weeping children, things he'd once wished his *nonna* had said to him when he was small and he'd skinned his knee or bloodied his nose, except this wasn't a bloody knee or nose, he thought, as he dug in his pocket and produced the ugly corpse.

The nurse grimaced; one of the physicians barked out a command, and Dante's heart turned over when the nurse appeared with a tiny needle and reached for Sam's hand.

"Shh, *bambina*," he whispered, "everything will be all right."

But Sam was past listening. Her little body arched; Dante cursed as a convulsion tore through her.

"Do something," he snarled.

"Wait outside," the doctor snapped.

Dante flashed him a look the man would never forget. "I will not leave my baby," he said.

He didn't. Not until Sam finally opened her eyes and looked at him.

"Da-Tay," she whispered, and for the first time since his mother had left him, Dante wept.

IT TOOK TWO HOURS and a dozen calls to the house by the sea before Tally answered the phone.

She was, as Dante had anticipated, frantic.

"Dante! Dear God, where are you? Where is Samantha? I came home and the place was empty and—"

He interrupted. Told her everything was fine, that they were at the hospital, in the emergency room. Lied and said he'd let his worry over a little bug bite get out of hand. He didn't want her to know the truth until he could take her in his arms and hold her and she could see for herself that the crisis was over.

He was waiting at the big double doors of the emergency room when she came flying through them.

"Where's my baby?"

Dante caught her in his arms. "She's fine, *cara*."

"Tell me the truth. My baby—"

"Tally." He held her by the shoulders, brought his eyes level with hers. "I would never lie to you. Never."

She nodded, though he could feel her tremble in his embrace. Slowly, carefully, he explained what had happened. When she swayed, he gathered her against him, rocked her gently until she pushed her hands against his chest and looked into his eyes.

"Where is she?"

He kept his arm around her, let his strength seep into her as he led her to Sam's room. The room was private; so was the nurse who sat beside the baby in the white crib, peacefully sleeping. The danger was past but the IV was still in her arm.

Tally bent over the crib and put her hand on her daughter's back. Tears fell from her eyes.

"My baby," she whispered, "oh, my sweet little girl! I could have lost you."

"Your husband did all the right things, Mrs. Russo," the nurse said softly. "Without his quick thinking, things would have been much worse."

Tally looked at the woman. "But he isn't—"

Dante slid his arm around her shoulders. "Let's let Sam sleep, *cara*. Come into the hall and we can talk."

Bewildered, Tally followed him from the room. "She thinks you and I are married?"

"I don't know the laws here, *cara*. But I remember reading about a child somewhere who died because a hospital wouldn't provide emergency treatment without the permission of a parent." He clasped her shoulders. "I wasn't going to run that risk. Not with our little girl."

Tally swallowed hard. *Our little girl. Our little girl.*

"Don't look at me that way, *cara*. I had no choice. Our Samantha—"

It was her fault, all of it. She had denied Dante knowledge of his child, denied Sam her father. And now, dear God, and now Sam might have died if Dante hadn't thought quickly—

"Tally."

She looked up at him. His face was drawn. He had gone through so much today for a child he didn't know was his, a child he loved.

"Tally." Dante paused. "I know my timing is bad but—*cara*, I want to marry you. And I want to adopt Sam. I want to be her father."

Tears swam in Tally's eyes. "Oh, Dante…"

"I love you. And I love her, as much as if she were my daughter."

Tally began to weep. There was no hiding her secret, not anymore.

"Dante," she said brokenly, "Sam *is* your daughter!"

There was a long silence, broken only by the sound of Dante's breathing and Tally's sobs. When he finally spoke, his voice was without inflection.

"What do you mean, Sam is my daughter?"

"I should have told you. I wanted to tell you—"

She gasped as his hands bit into her shoulders. "Tell me what?"

"There was no other man. I made it up. Samantha is—she's your child."

Moments, an eternity, slipped by. Tally waited, trying to read Dante's face, to see something of what would come next.

"Let me make sure I understand this. You didn't sleep with someone else."

"No."

"You didn't get pregnant by another man."

"I know I should have told you, but—"

"You knew you were pregnant, and you left me anyway?"

"Dante. Please. Listen to what I'm saying. I knew

you'd grown tired of me. How could I have told you I was having a baby?"

"My baby." His voice was like a whip; he caught her wrists and pushed her back against the wall. "*My* baby!"

"It isn't that simple!"

"On the contrary, Taylor. It's brutally simple. You became pregnant with my child and didn't tell me. You were going to raise her to think she had no father."

Tally wrenched her hands free and slapped them over her ears. "Stop it!"

"You were going to raise Samantha—my daughter—as I was raised. Fatherless. Impoverished."

"It wasn't like that, damn it! I did what I thought was right."

"For who? Surely not for Samantha. And not for me."

"Remember when I said I wanted to talk to you? It was about this. About you and Sam. But I had to wait for the right time."

He gave a hollow laugh. "Another lie. How many more will you tell before I know the entire truth?"

Tally stared up into her lover's enraged eyes. He was right. It was time for the truth. All of it.

"No more lies," she said, her voice trembling. "Here's the truth. Sam is yours. There was never anyone else. And I left you—I left you because I knew I'd fallen in love with you."

"Such a pretty story."

"I swear it's true! I still love you. I always will."

"As soon as my daughter is fully recovered," he said, as if she hadn't spoken, "we'll fly back to New York."

"Damn you, Dante! Listen to me!"

"You will move back into the guest suite. I'll permit

that because I don't want my child to be traumatized by too many changes all at once."

A cold knot of fear gripped Tally's stomach. "What does that mean?"

Dante smiled thinly.

"It means," he said silkily, "that Samantha is mine. That you stole her from me. That you are an unfit mother." He paused. "And that I intend to gain custody—sole custody—of her."

"No!" Tally's voice rose in horror. "You can't take her from me. No court will permit it!"

Dante ignored her, walked to the room where Sam lay sleeping and sat down in a chair beside the crib. So much for love. For putting your heart in someone's hands. For being foolish enough to think life was ever anything but a cruel joke.

He took his cell phone from his pocket, called his attorney, cut through the man's perfunctory greeting and told him he'd just learned he was the father of a two-year-old child.

The lawyer, who dealt with several wealthy clients, cut to the chase.

"How much does the woman want?"

"You misunderstand me," Dante said. "I don't want to deny my paternity of the child, I want to claim her. I want full custody. Will that be a problem?"

He listened, answered a couple of questions, then smiled.

There were times having money, power and the right connections paid off.

CHAPTER TWELVE

MOMENTS LATER, TALLY entered the room.

Dante, still seated beside the crib and the sleeping baby, looked at the nurse.

"Please take your dinner break now."

He spoke politely, but that didn't lessen his tone of command. The woman left without a backward glance. Tally looked at him, but he didn't acknowledge her presence.

Anyone looking at him would assume he was angry.

She knew better. He was furious. And it frightened her. Dante was a powerful adversary in any situation. Now he would be formidable.

But he wouldn't win. She would do whatever it took to keep her child and defeat him, and that meant facing up to him, starting now.

She moved the nurse's abandoned chair to the other side of the crib and sat down. Her face softened as she looked at her little girl, so peacefully asleep.

Samantha was hers.

No court in the land would separate a mother from her child, not even to satisfy Dante Russo. None, she thought…and maybe because she wished she really believed it, she spoke the words aloud.

"You won't win," she said.

He looked at her, his eyes empty. "Of course I will."

Her face paled. Good. He was happy to see it. She deserved what would come next. She had brought it on herself with her lies.

His attorney was already earning his million-dollar-a-year retainer, drawing up motions and citing precedents even though the hour was late and Christmas was only a couple of days away.

Dante had no doubt as to which of them would gain custody. Tally had apple pie and motherhood on her side, but he had the things that really mattered.

What a fool he'd been, imagining himself in love. He almost laughed. He, of all people, knew that the word had no meaning. His mother had claimed to love him, right up to the day she kissed him, told him to be a good boy, and vanished. His *nonna* had claimed to love him, too, and proved it by beating the crap out of him at every opportunity until he finally ran away.

Emotion was weakness. Self-discipline was strength. This woman had made him forget that, but he would not make the same mistake again.

The one thing he couldn't understand was why she had kept her pregnancy from him. He was rich. She could have milked him for a lot of money. He knew men who'd had that happen to them. A woman got pregnant, deliberately pregnant, and dipped her manicured hands into a man's bank account.

Anyone could see that Tally could have used the cash. The old house in Vermont, the business she'd attempted... An infusion of dollars would have changed her life.

All right. She had not been after his money. He had to admit that. And he had to admit that she seemed to be a good mother.

Why, then, had she lied? Why had she left him?

Because she loved him. That was what she'd said.

What a joke!

A woman who loved a man didn't run from him. She didn't give birth to his child and tell him the child was someone else's. *Dio,* the anger and pain that had caused him. The nights he'd lain awake, held Tally in his arms, tried not to wonder if she were dreaming of him or of her other lover.

His mouth thinned.

It was some consolation, at least, knowing she had not belonged to anyone else. That she had been his. Only his. That no one else had made love to her, held her close, felt the whisper of her breath against his throat while she slept in his arms.

He'd blanked his mind to the rest. To what she'd looked like when she was pregnant. Now, knowing Sam was his, that was impossible to do.

Her breasts would have been full, the skin translucent over the delicate tracery of her veins. Her belly would have been round, lush with the life they'd created. She had denied him the wonder of those months. The feel of his child, kicking in her mother's womb. The moment of his child's entry into the world.

All those signs, the proof of their love...

Except, it had never been love.

Never. Love was just a polite four-letter word men

and women used in mixed company. Taylor's lies were the issue here, not love.

He'd had the right to know the truth. She should have told him.

He looked up. Tally sat with her head bowed. "You should have told me," he said coldly.

She raised her eyes to his.

"You're right. I should have."

"But you didn't."

"No. I didn't. I've tried to explain, to say I'm sorry—"

"I'm not interested in apologies or explanations."

She gave a sad little laugh. "No. You're only interested in you. That's one of the reasons I didn't tell you I was pregnant. I was afraid you'd react exactly this way, as if our baby's existence concerned only you."

"You're good at making excuses."

"Not as good as you are at feeling nothing for anyone but yourself." Her voice trembled. "I think you do care for Samantha, though. And that surprises me."

"A compliment, *cara*. I can hardly bear it."

"Dante. Don't take her from me. I know you want to hurt me, but you'll hurt her, too."

"Hurt her?" His lips drew back from his teeth. "You have nothing. I have everything. I'll give my daughter a life you can only imagine."

"She's my daughter, too. And what she needs is love. It's what everyone needs. How can you not understand that?"

"*Love*," he said, his mouth twisting, "is a word without meaning. *Honesty. Responsibility.* Those are words that matter. How can you not understand that?"

Then he folded his arms, fixed his eyes on the sleeping baby and ignored Tally completely.

DAWN HAD JUST TOUCHED the sky with a delicate pink blush when Samantha stirred.

"Mama?"

Tally, who'd fallen into a fitful sleep, sprang to her feet, but she was too late. Dante had already leaned into the crib and lifted the baby into his arms.

"Bella figlia," he said huskily, *"buon giorno."*

Sam grinned. "Da-Tay," she babbled, and wrapped her arms around his neck.

Tally felt her throat tighten. All the time she'd been pregnant, the months and years after, she'd never pictured this. Dante and Samantha as father and daughter. She'd never dreamed of this softness, this sweetness in her lover.

The door opened. The physician who'd treated Sam stepped into the room.

"Well, look at this! It doesn't take a trained eye to see that our patient's made a full recovery."

"Thank you, Doctor. For everything."

"My pleasure, Mr. Russo. Just let me give your little girl the once-over and you can take her home."

"To New York?"

"I'd wait a couple of days, just to be on the safe side." He grinned. "Quite a hardship, having to spend Christmas in the Caribbean, huh, folks?"

Tally made a choked sound. Dante forced a smile.

"We'll manage," he said.

Tally hoped he was right.

COEXISTING in a three-level penthouse, as they'd initially done, was simple.

Coexisting in a one-level house built to take full advantage of the sun was not.

Rooms opened into rooms; doors were almost non-existent. Tally moved her things into the third bedroom, but it was impossible to walk to the kitchen or Sam's room without running into Dante.

"Excuse me," she said, at the beginning.

After a while, she stopped saying it. What was there to apologize for? He was as much in her way as she was in his.

And how did he manage to get to Sam's side so quickly? All the baby had to do was whimper and Dante, damn him, was there.

Tally told herself she'd at least have the pleasure of watching him suffer through the horrors of a full diaper but apparently he'd mastered Diaper 101 on his own. All right, she thought with petty satisfaction, at least he wouldn't know how to mash a banana just the way Sam liked it—and she was right. He didn't.

It didn't matter.

Her sweet little traitor liked Dante's method just fine. She liked everything he did, including taking her for hand-in-hand walks along the beach, the warm water lapping at her ankles.

When Tally attempted the same thing, Sam shrieked with horror.

Dante could charm any woman he set his eyes on, including two-year-old females.

But he couldn't charm Tally. Not that he tried. He looked right through her. That was fine. She'd gone back to hating him. She'd never let her little girl be raised by such a cold-hearted tyrant, never mind the performance he was putting on with Sam, never mind the way his face lit each time the baby toddled toward him…

Never mind the numbing sense of sorrow in her own heart at glimpses of what might have been.

As midnight approached, with Sam sound asleep and the house silent, Tally was close to tears, but it wasn't over Dante.

Never over him.

"Never," Tally whispered, and wept as if her heart might break in half.

TALLY'S SOFT SOBS carried through the walls.

Lying on his bed, arms folded beneath his head, Dante stared up at the dark ceiling. Let her cry, he thought coldly. For all he gave a damn, she could cry enough salt tears to fill the sea.

After a long time, the sound of her weeping grew softer, then stopped. A muscle in his jaw flexed. Good. Now, at least, he might get some sleep.

Half an hour later, he sat up.

To hell with sleep. He was going crazy, trapped in a house that was rapidly becoming a prison. He pulled on a pair of shorts, opened the patio doors and strode over the beach until he reached the surf.

The moon, full and round, was bright enough to carve shadows into the sand. Dante's mouth thinned. It was the kind of night you saw on picture postcards. The endless stretch of sand. The white ruffle of the surf. The dark sea stretching to the horizon under the elegantly cool eye of the moon.

Once, he'd considered buying a house in these islands. He'd even mentioned it to Taylor. The idea had come from out of nowhere...or maybe not. Maybe he'd thought of the beauty of this place because Taylor was so beautiful. Because, fool that he was, he'd imagined he was feeling something for her he'd never felt for another woman.

He'd stepped back from that precipice.

And here he was, three years later, with her in the very setting he'd imagined, except all he wanted was to get away from her and return to New York.

Dio, the irony of it!

Dante kicked at the sand as he walked slowly along the beach.

A beautiful island. A beautiful woman, but what good was her beauty if she had no heart? Not when it came to him.

And why should that mean a damn anyway, when he'd never thought the human heart was responsible for anything more than pumping blood through the body?

Wrong, he thought, tilting back his head and staring blindly at the moon. Dead wrong, and it had taken a two-year-old imp to teach him the lesson.

A painful lesson.

For the first time in his life, he'd begun to think about a different existence from any he'd ever known. A house in the country. A dog, a couple of cats, a station wagon. A little girl to run to the door when she heard his key in the lock and maybe a little boy, too…

And a wife, to step into his embrace.

Not just a wife. Tally. His Tally. Because that was how he thought of her, how he'd always thought of her, even three years ago…

What was that?

Dante cocked his head. Music? Chimes. No. Not chimes. Bells. Church bells. Of course. It must be midnight, and this was Christmas Eve.

He swallowed hard. So what? Christmas was for fools. A holiday that celebrated a miracle, except miracles were in painfully short supply in today's world.

When was the last time he'd seen anything remotely like a miracle?

When was the last time he'd held Tally in his arms?

The sound of the bells came to him again, filled with poignancy and hope that floated on the soft sea breeze. Dante swallowed again but he couldn't ease the constriction in his throat.

"Tally," he whispered, and the name was sweeter than the music of the bells.

Tally was his miracle. She always had been.

And he'd turned his back on that miracle, ruined his one chance at love, at happiness, out of pride, arrogance, all the things she'd accused him of, rather than admit the truth.

He loved Tally. Now, three years ago, forever. He adored her.

And he knew exactly why she'd left him.

He *had* been about to end their affair, just as she'd said, and it hadn't had a damned thing to do with boredom. The truth was the great Dante Russo had been terrified of putting his heart in a woman's hands, of saying, *Here I am, cara. A man, nothing more. A man who loves you and can only hope you love him in return because without you, I am nothing. My life is nothing....*

Dante took a shuddering breath.

"Tally," he whispered, and turned toward the house.

TALLY LAY HUDDLED in her bed, eyes hot and gritty with tears.

Ridiculous, wasn't it? To weep over Dante? He wasn't worth it. Not anymore.

He had shown his true colors today. He was the cold, brutal, arrogant tyrant she'd always called him...

Tally rolled onto her back and stared up at the dark ceiling. No. That wasn't true. Dante had been wonderful today, quick and courageous and tender with Sam, and with her...

Until she'd told him what she should have told him a very long time ago.

She could be honest about this, at least. Dante wasn't a tyrant, he was a man in pain. She had told him a lie that had cut to the bone. Now he was hurting. And a man like Dante Russo knew only one way to deal with pain.

He struck at its cause.

And she—she was the cause.

A sob caught in Tally's throat and she rolled over and buried her face in the already-damp pillow.

If only she'd told him the truth that day in Vermont, when he'd first seen Sam. If only she'd said, "Dante, this is your child. I kept her from you and I kept myself from you, too, because—because I loved you. Because I knew I'd die if you turned away from me."

Would he have laughed? Or would he have opened his arms to her? She'd never know. It was too late. She'd finally told him the truth, that Sam was his and that she loved him, but it didn't matter.

He wanted Sam, not her. And she couldn't blame him for that. Her lies had destroyed everything.

Too late, the beat of her heart said, too late, too late, too—

What was that?

Tally sat up, head cocked. Bells? Yes. Bells, chiming sweetly through the night. Why would bells be...

Of course.

It was Christmas. Christmas! The bells were heralding the start of the holiday, singing of joy, of wonder…

Of miracles.

Tears streamed down Tally's face. She'd had her own miracle. A man. Proud. Strong. Protective and, yes, loving. And she'd let that miracle slip through her fingers out of cowardice. She'd been afraid to tell him about Sam.

And terrified to tell him about herself, that she loved him, that she'd always love him, until it was too late.

Almost too late, she thought, and drew a ragged breath.

Tally threw back the covers and rose from the bed. Her footsteps were hesitant at first but they quickened as she ran from room to room.

"Dante," she said brokenly, "my beloved, where are you?"

The bells rang out again, just as she hurried into the sitting room. A beam of ivory moonlight illuminated the French doors that led to the beach. Tally flung them open—

And saw Dante, just as he turned toward the house.

"Dante," she said, and she began to run across the sand, "Dante…"

Moonlight touched his face. She saw love, understanding, the same hope that burned in her heart, and she flew into his embrace and clung to him.

"I heard the bells," she said, crying and laughing at the same time, kissing his mouth as she rose to him, luxuriating in the racing beat of his heart. "I heard them calling and I thought, I can't lose him again, I can't, I can't, I can't—"

"I love you," Dante said fiercely, cupping her face in

his hands. "I've always loved you, *inamorata,* but I was too proud—and too afraid of needing you—to admit it."

"And I love you," Tally said, "I always have. It's why I left you three years ago. The thought of having you end things between us was more than I could bear."

"I was a fool, *cara,*" he said, tightening his arms around her. "How could a man end what is destined to last through eternity?"

Tally laughed through her tears. "Is that all?"

He smiled, too. And then his mouth was on hers, the taste of her tears was on his lips, and as he lifted her into his arms and carried her to the house, the bells rang out, telling the world that miracles are always possible.

All you have to do is believe.

SOMETIMES, HAVING WEALTH and power and all the right connections really did pay off.

They flew back to New York early in the morning the next day, Tally wearing the diamond solitaire Dante had bought for her in the Caribbean.

"It's beautiful," she whispered, when he slipped the ring on her finger.

"Not as beautiful as you," he said, and kissed her.

All the municipal offices were closed, but such details weren't enough to put a crimp in the plans of Dante Russo.

"I know someone who knows someone who knows someone," he said, laughing when Tally rolled her eyes.

"Such arrogance," she said, but her smile, her voice, her eyes shone with love.

By noon, they had a wedding license and a judge who said he'd be happy to marry them in Dante's penthouse.

By one, the penthouse was filled with Christmas

garlands. Mistletoe hung from every doorway. Dante loved catching Tally under the mistletoe, whirling her in a circle and kissing her.

The enormous sitting room was filled with baskets of crimson and white poinsettias. Holly leaves, bright with berries, lay draped over the top of the fireplace mantel. But the room's centerpiece was a blue spruce so tall its branches reached the ceiling.

The tree was beautiful.

It filled the air with its fragrance; it glowed with what Tally was sure were a thousand white fairy lights. The flames on the hearth in the wall-long fireplace danced on the gleaming surfaces of the gold and silver balls that hung from the tree. Gaily wrapped packages spilled from under the branches, though Sam, squealing with delight, had already opened most of hers.

Champagne was chilling in silver buckets; caviar sat in a silver dish. Everything was perfect...and a little before two, the doorman brought up an enormous white box. Inside was a magnificent gown of lace and seed pearls, straight from the atelier of a world-famous designer.

It was the sort of gown princesses wear in the fairy tales little girls read.

Except, Tally thought when she finally stood beside her gorgeous groom and looked up into his eyes, except, this was no fairy tale.

This was real. It was true love, and it would last forever.

"Do you take this woman," the judge intoned, and Dante short-circuited things by saying "Yes."

The perfect P.A., who was one of the guests, laughed. So did Mrs. Tipton and so did Samantha, who she held against her bosom.

Dante brought his bride's hand to his lips. They smiled into each other's eyes. Then they gave the judge all their attention. Slowly, and with deep meaning, they took the vows that would forever unite them.

Moments later, they were husband and wife. Dante gathered his bride to him and kissed her again.

"I will love you forever, *inamorata*," he said softly.

Tally smiled through tears of happiness. "As I will love you," she whispered.

"Me, too," Sam said.

Everyone laughed as the baby made her pronouncement.

"Down," she told Mrs. Tipton, with all the imperiousness of a two-year-old. She toddled to her parents and held up her arms. "Up," she commanded.

Dante, a man who never took orders from anyone, happily took this one and settled his daughter into the curve of his arm.

"Mama," Sam said, touching a chubby hand to Tally's cheek.

She looked at Dante, who smiled and waited for her to call him Da-Tay.

But she didn't.

Instead, she put a little hand on each side of his face and said, "Dada."

Dante's eyes filled. He looked at his wife, and Tally smiled.

"Merry Christmas, beloved," she whispered.

"*Buon natale, inamorata*," he said softly.

Their daughter laughed, and flung her arms around them both.

REQUEST YOUR FREE BOOKS!

2 FREE NOVELS PLUS 2 FREE GIFTS!

HARLEQUIN®

Blaze

Red-hot reads!

YES! Please send me 2 FREE Harlequin® Blaze® novels and my 2 FREE gifts. After receiving them, if I don't wish to receive any more books, I can return the shipping statement marked "cancel." If I don't cancel, I will receive 6 brand-new novels every month and be billed just $3.99 per book in the U.S., or $4.47 per book in Canada, plus 25¢ shipping and handling per book and applicable taxes, if any*. That's a savings of at least 15% off the cover price! I understand that accepting the 2 free books and gifts places me under no obligation to buy anything. I can always return a shipment and cancel at any time. Even if I never buy another book from Harlequin, the two free books and gifts are mine to keep forever.

151 HDN EF3W   351 HDN EF3X

Name	(PLEASE PRINT)

Address	Apt.

City	State/Prov.	Zip/Postal Code

Signature (if under 18, a parent or guardian must sign).

Mail to Harlequin Reader Service®:

IN U.S.A.	**IN CANADA**
P.O. Box 1867	P.O. Box 609
Buffalo, NY	Fort Erie, Ontario
14240-1867	L2A 5X3

Not valid to current Harlequin Blaze subscribers.

Want to try two free books from another line?
Call 1-800-873-8635 or visit www.morefreebooks.com.

* Terms and prices subject to change without notice. NY residents add applicable sales tax. Canadian residents will be charged applicable provincial taxes and GST. This offer is limited to one order per household. All orders subject to approval. Credit or debit balances in a customer's account(s) may be offset by any other outstanding balance owed by or to the customer. Please allow 4 to 6 weeks for delivery.

HB06